"I need a regular con____
some of the heat off____
of the Year thing," D____

"Someone to accompany me to functions. It'll be good publicity for you, too. And if they do find out anything about what happened in Paris, my influence with the media here could come in handy. As for finance—I have an empty room that you can use rent-free to get your business started."

Mariel was still stuck on *regular.* "How regular are we talking?"

His eyes were like charcoal now, and intense. "You'll move in with me—"

"Whoa. Hold it. *Move in with you?* So in the public's eyes we're a couple?"

"Lovers," he corrected.

Heat spurted through her veins at the mental image. "So we've gone from companion and a couple of dates to *lovers?*"

His gaze remained steady on hers. "I won't pretend not to want you in my bed, Mariel."

"What makes you think I'd want to be there?" she retorted.

What made her think she could resist?

When not teaching or writing, **ANNE OLIVER** loves nothing more than escaping into a book. She keeps a box of tissues handy—her favorite stories are intense, passionate, against-all-odds romances. Eight years ago she began creating her own characters in paranormal and time-travel adventures, before turning to contemporary romance. Other interests include quilting, astronomy, all things Scottish and eating anything she doesn't have to cook. Sharing her characters' journeys with readers all over the world is a privilege…and a dream come true. Anne lives in Adelaide, South Australia, and has two adult children. Visit her Web site at www.anne-oliver.com. She loves to hear from readers. E-mail her at anne@anne-oliver.com.

MISTRESS: AT WHAT PRICE?
ANNE OLIVER

~ P.S. I'm Pregnant! ~

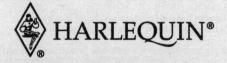

HARLEQUIN®

TORONTO • NEW YORK • LONDON
AMSTERDAM • PARIS • SYDNEY • HAMBURG
STOCKHOLM • ATHENS • TOKYO • MILAN • MADRID
PRAGUE • WARSAW • BUDAPEST • AUCKLAND

Recycling programs
for this product may
not exist in your area.

ISBN-13: 978-0-373-52776-2

MISTRESS: AT WHAT PRICE?

First North American Publication 2010.

Copyright © 2010 by Anne Oliver.

www.eHarlequin.com

Printed in U.S.A.

MISTRESS:
AT WHAT PRICE?

With a big thank-you to my critique buddies,
Kathy, Sharon and Linda, for helping me
bring out the best in Mariel and Dane's story.

Thanks also to my editor Meg Lewis
for her patience and advice
during the revision process.

CHAPTER ONE

'REMIND me again why I dragged my jet-lagged body to a wedding with you when I could be sleeping it off in the comfort of my own bed?'

Mariel Davenport glanced at her sister Phoebe over the obligatory glass of champagne—except Mariel's glass sparkled with mineral water. After the stress of packing and avoiding the press, then the long-haul flight from Paris, the last thing she needed was alcohol.

She skimmed the elite crowd, dripping with diamonds and couture and French perfume. Some she knew; most were strangers. Ten years away was a long time.

Phoebe flashed a smile, brown eyes sparkling. 'Because you're my big sister and you love me, and we haven't seen each other since that Mediterranean cruise three years ago.'

Mariel arched a brow. 'Not because your boyfriend left you in the—?'

'*Ex*-boyfriend,' Phoebe snarled, all humour extinguished. She topped up her champagne flute from the bottle on the nearby table with a sharp chink of glass on crystal. 'Kyle's history.' She tossed back a mouthful of bubbly in disgust. 'Men. Who'd trust them?'

The words pierced the thin armour Mariel had struggled to wrap around herself since leaving Paris. 'Who indeed?'

Phoebe's eyes widened in obvious dismay. 'Oh, Mari, I'm sorry…'

'Don't be. I was a fool; it won't happen again.' She bit down on the inside of her lower lip. Hadn't she made that very same vow once before? Right here in her home town?

'That's the spirit.' Phoebe's firm nod had her blonde bangs bouncing. 'New Year's resolution: no men. Until the next full moon at least.' She grinned, then tucked her hand into the crook of Mariel's arm as the band struck up a popular party hit. 'Let's mingle.' The happy couple had left but the revelry lived on. 'Or we could dance,' she suggested. 'It'll take your mind off things.'

Mariel shook her head. 'You know I love nothing better than a good party, but not tonight.' What sane people would choose New Year's Day to get married anyway? She raised her glass and pointed it towards the crowd congregating on the makeshift dance floor beyond the open French doors of the luxurious old Adelaide Hills mansion. 'You go ahead. I'm fine. I'll just loiter here a while.'

'Are you sure?'

'Positive.' She fixed a smile on her lips and shooed Phoebe away. 'Go.'

Mariel watched her sister thread her way through the colourful crowd, her silk and diamonds shimmering beneath the heavy chandelier. Only then did she allow herself a much-needed sigh. Phoebe knew nothing of the mess Mariel had left behind in Paris except that it

was over between her and French fashion photographer
Luc Girard, her business partner of seven years and
lover for the past five.

He was probably the reason she'd thrown up—
twice—somewhere over China. She massaged the heel
of her hand over the affected area. The organza of the
latest and probably last addition to her after-five
wardrobe shifted beneath her palm.

Turning her back to the room, she sipped water and
studied the guests through the gilt-edged mirror over
the mantelpiece.

The bride's parents, who'd spared no expense for
their daughter's special day, were conversing with
another wealthy Hills couple near the floor-to-ceiling
ice sculpture, now dripping in Adelaide's January heat.

Was that little Johnny…? What was his last name?
Mariel frowned at the blond guy, trying to remember.
Not so little now, she thought with a twinge of nostal-
gia. And there was nothing she liked better than a guy
in a well-tailored suit. As her gaze moved on, she
realised several of the well-suited men were eyeing her
up. And not-so-little Johnny What's-his-name was
headed her way. Great. Just what she *didn't* need.

She knew she attracted men. With her face on the cover
of Europe's top magazines, and becoming a familiar face
in Australia, it was inevitable. But tonight she could have
done without the attention. Especially tonight, since she'd
just sworn off men for life. Another sigh slipped past her
lips as she automatically checked her lipstick in the mirror,
straightened her shoulders and turned, smile back in place.

Well, surprise, surprise. Daniel Huntington the Third,
who refused to answer to anything but Dane, leaned a

shoulder against the doorway and watched Mariel Davenport hold court, her little flock of male admirers clustered around her, apparently hanging on every word that spilled from those luscious coral lips.

She was the last person he'd expected to see here this evening. Nor had he anticipated the quick punch to his solar plexus as he cast a critical eye over the breezy black halterneck number, with its plummeting neckline and incy-wincy skirt. He was pretty sure if he stood close enough and let his eyes skim casually down he'd see her navel.

Not that he intended to stand that close. With his six-foot-three advantage he could see her well enough from here. He thought he might just be able to smell the perfume she used to wear—that hint of black roses and sweet sin seemed to waft across the few feet between them. Alluring, seductive. It suited her, from the tips of her raven-black hair, piled on top of her head, to the soles of her perfectly pedicured feet and shiny stiletto sandals.

He couldn't see her feet, of course, or those mile-long legs that had her topping out at nearly six foot, but he knew her well enough. First class all the way.

She hadn't noticed him yet, but he lifted his beer in mock salute, then poured a fortifying mouthful of the cool bitter brew down his suddenly dry throat.

Was she with someone? he wondered. Her French lover? Odd how his fingernails bit into his palms at the thought. He'd been fine about that little detail until a moment ago.

Until he'd seen her again in all that glorious flesh.

But, no, she must have come alone—because if she'd had a partner Dane was pretty sure the man would be attached to her side like some fashion accessory.

He flexed the fingers of his free hand, flicked them against his thigh, and watched her flash that cover-winning smile at her fans. The one thing Mariel loved was attention, be it personal or the camera. And from what he'd heard about her career over the past years, and seen in the latest beauty magazine that her sister had touted, the camera loved Mariel.

Fashion designer turned photographic model.

He considered speaking to her, but he wasn't about to become one of her fawning admirers. Good grief, a couple of those guys had been exploring Play Dough and finger paint when she'd been experimenting with make-up and mobile phones. Did they not realise? He expelled a harsh breath through his nostrils. He could wait.

'Ah, here's our very own newly announced *Babe* magazine's Bachelor of the Year.' Justin Talbot materialised beside him. 'I was wondering where you'd got to, my friend.'

'Looks like you found me.' Dane glanced his way, mentally shaking his head at the snazzy dove-grey waistcoat, matching tie and wing-tip collar Justin's new wife had obviously picked out. Dane didn't believe in conforming to dress code unless it was for a funeral.

'You've done us proud,' said Justin, clapping a hand on Dane's shoulder.

'Easy for you to say.' Dane scowled, his gaze unerringly finding Mariel again. 'You dobbed me in.'

As if he needed more women hounding him. Since he'd won the title he'd grown very weary of the relentless parade of would-be starlets clamouring for his attention.

'Think of it as doing your bit for charity,' Justin said.

'There are better ways to raise funds,' Dane muttered. 'And the press is having a field-day.'

'What did you expect? Millionaire businessman, founder of OzRemote *and* eligible bachelor. Hey…it's Mariel Davenport.'

Dane felt Justin's voice switch from jovial to slightly breathless like a prickle between his shoulderblades. He shrugged the feeling off. 'So it appears.'

'Jee-ee-z. Looking good, Mariel,' Justin murmured. 'Even better than that photo spread Phoebe showed us. She hasn't been back in…how long? What's she doing at Carl and Amy's wedding?'

'Ten years.' And five months. 'And your guess is as good as mine,' he muttered, frowning into his amber liquid.

'Wasn't she living with some French guy?'

'Yep.'

'You spoken to her yet?'

'Nope.' Sweat trickled down Dane's back, making his shirt stick. He tossed back the remainder of his beer and thought about stepping outside for some fresh air. The atmosphere was stifling in here, even with the air-con working overtime.

'Why not?' Justin queried. 'You two were pretty close. I remember—'

'That was a long time ago.'

A lifetime ago… The night before she'd left for overseas. In her bedroom, the full moon filtering through the open window, its silver light bathing her milk-white skin, her eyes black pools of wonder, gazing up at him…

Dane shifted his stance, cleared his throat as every hot-blooded cell south of his larynx mobilised. 'You right for a drink?'

'We're leaving in a moment, Cass has an early start

tomorrow. I'm going to say hi to Mariel before we go; want to join me?'

Dane shook his head. 'I'll catch up with her later.' He turned and pointed himself in the direction of the nearest drinks waiter.

But, damn, he couldn't let it go. His head swivelled in time to see Justin plant a kiss full on Mariel's smiling lips. He knew it meant nothing more than what it was— a welcome home—but a sudden tension locked Dane's jaw, making his teeth clench. His fingers tightened around his glass.

He watched his mate whisper something close to her ear and Mariel turned slowly to look Dane's way. So slowly—or maybe it was just that the moment seemed to crawl to a stop—that he had time to experience, in graphic detail, the full effect of that face, that attention, focused wholly on him.

The way the high cheekbones flushed with colour, the flutter of long black lashes as she blinked those emerald eyes at him, just once. The way her glossy lips parted slightly—in surprise or dismay?—then lifted infinitesimally at the corners, resembling something approaching warmth.

Whatever—it faded like a rose in winter, no doubt as she took in his rigid jaw and neutral stare. Because, frankly, he couldn't seem to drum up anything else. She lifted a hand, let it hover a moment before she smoothed a non-existent strand of hair behind her ear.

Her eyes were still locked with his. Until her gaze lifted to his hair. And, yeah, some might say it needed a trim. Her nostrils flared slightly as her gaze shifted to his open-necked shirt. His throat prickled; his Adam's apple bobbed. Hell. He was glad he didn't have a woman, particularly an ex-fashion designer, telling him how he should dress.

And thanks to Justin's intervention he had no alternative—manners dictated he at least speak to her. Forcibly unclenching his teeth and loosening his grip on the glass, he started forward.

Mariel watched Dane Huntington saunter towards her, his casual, almost arrogant manner all too familiar. Whatever Justin was saying—if he was saying anything at all—faded. Her stomach juddered once, as if she'd hit more of that air turbulence she'd experienced on the final approach into Adelaide.

Phoebe, where are you? Get me out of here, she pleaded silently. She should have known she'd bump into him sooner or later, but Dane was the last man she wanted to face right now, with her body clock out of sync and her digestive system doing nasty things to her insides.

She'd wanted to look her best when she saw him again. Show him what he'd missed out on all those years ago, when she'd been a naïve seventeen-year-old who'd thought the young Dane Huntington was her sun and moon and everything in between.

Well, she wasn't so naïve now, even if it had taken every one of those ten years. Seconds ticked by, but they felt like minutes. His cool grey gaze remained fused with hers, no hint of a smile on those beautiful lips. Lifting her chin, she sucked in her stomach and eye-balled him boldly as he drew nearer.

Dark hair with glints of auburn covered his ears and carelessly kissed the back of his neck. Some things hadn't changed, she thought with attempted disdain.

And he still scorned traditional dress code. He was tie-less. His black collarless shirt with white stitching along the seams was undone at the neck and revealed tanned skin and a smattering of dark hair.

The fashion designer inside her winced. Black jeans, to one of Adelaide's Society Weddings of the Year, for heaven's sake? But, to her chagrin, the wholly inappropriate image made her thighs melt and her pulse do a strange little blip.

She straightened, clutching her glass tighter to hide the fact that her fingers were trembling, and said, 'Hello, there,' before he opened his mouth. 'Happy New Year.'

She did *not* lean in for a kiss.

'Mariel. Happy New Year to you, too. How long have you been back?'

'I flew in yesterday morning.'

'Just in time for Carl and Amy's big day.'

His whisky-on-velvet voice flowed over her and he smiled—finally—and her pulse did another of those little blips. With her height she didn't often experience men looking down at her and it made her feel delicate. And feminine.

She stiffened. She didn't *want* to feel delicate and feminine with Dane Huntington. Ever again. But—and how crazy was this?—she wanted him to see her that way.

To remember… Did he remember?

How could he forget?

'Coincidentally Dane mentioned you just the other day,' Justin said, and Mariel saw the familiar little tic in Dane's jaw.

'Oh?' Dane had been talking about *her*? 'Why was that?'

'My wife, Cass, and I are thinking about going to Europe in October, and since you live in Paris he thought maybe you could give us the guided tour.'

'Did he?' She speared Dane with the pointy end of her gaze. 'He didn't try to look me up when he was there. When was it—five years ago, Dane? Mum mentioned it in an e-mail.'

'It was business, Mariel,' he said. 'There wasn't time for sightseeing. Or anything else. It was in and out. What brings you home?'

'Family. I needed a break.'

'One would think if you wanted to be with family you'd have come a week earlier and celebrated Christmas with them.'

Oh. 'I'm ashamed to say I left it too late and the airlines were fully booked.' She refused to look away beneath his close scrutiny. Look away and he'd know she was lying.

'That's too bad.'

'I'm here now.'

'So you are,' he said lazily, eyes still locked on hers.

Justin, obviously feeling the weird tension, switched topics. 'Our Dane won *Babe*'s Bachelor of the Year contest.'

'Is that so?' Mariel lifted her glass and took a sip to soothe her throat, noting the dark look Dane flashed at the other man.

'You remember the one,' Justin went on. '*Babe* magazine runs it every year.'

'Ah, yes, *that* magazine,' she drawled, infusing her tone with a large dollop of sarcasm, and was rewarded with a flare of colour on Dane's cheekbones.

And what do you know? Dane Huntington, master

of cool, actually looked hot. The hot-and-bothered kind of hot. Amused, she watched his head tilt as he stretched his neck, as if easing the tension there. The smile that touched her lips was more of a smirk.

'The side benefits: dates with ten different babes.' Justin grinned, with the devil's glint in his eyes.

Mariel's stomach clenched around the image Justin provoked, but she held on to that smirk for all she was worth.

'Uh-oh, my wife's giving me the eye,' Justin said. 'I'll leave you two to catch up. Great seeing you again, Mariel.'

'You, too.' Mariel smiled at an attractive brunette watching them as Justin threaded his way in her direction, then turned back to Dane. 'So...*Babe*'s Bachelor of the Year, huh? How does it work again?'

'Like Jus told you,' he clipped. 'A bit of fun. And it's for a good cause. Charity fund-raiser. I need a refill— how about you?' Jutting his chin, he motioned her away from several interested onlookers towards a punchbowl in the middle of a table.

He ladled orange liquid into two crystal cups, offered her one. 'Thank you,' she said, careful to avoid contact with his fingers.

'You mean these *babes*—' Mariel drew the word out with sarcastic relish '—wherever they come from, they rate the contestants and the highest score wins? What are they scoring you on, I wonder?' She couldn't help the wicked smile...but inside, somewhere deep and almost forgotten, something hurt. 'I can't wait to see you on the cover of the magazine.'

He shook his head. 'It's not as bad as you think.'

'How bad am I thinking?'

'The date ends at the front door.'

Biting back resentment that she thought she'd got over years ago, she said, 'That'll be a novelty for you, then. I've heard you're a regular Casanova these days.'

His lips stretched into an indolent grin that didn't reach his eyes. 'Don't believe everything you hear.'

The back of her throat tickled at the sound of that lazy tone. She glanced down, flicking her eyes to his again before they had time to indulge in the snug fit of his jeans and the way his exclusive hand-made *casual* shirt clung to his chest, even if the seam was too narrow for his broad shoulders. 'If you're going to look the part you'll really have to update your wardrobe, or acquire a new tailor.'

'Ah, ever the fashion designer. And looking a million bucks tonight,' he said, his gaze skimming her body, just a tad longer than might be considered polite in company. 'One of your designs?'

She met his eyes, paused, smiling inwardly, then sipped her drink. 'No.' *Hah.* He obviously knew nothing about her designs.

'That's right—you're a photographer's model these days. I saw your picture in a magazine here a couple of months back. Phoebe showed us. Very nice.'

His gaze swept over her once more. Was he comparing her to his girlfriends? According to Phoebe's regular newsy e-mails from home, Dane enjoyed more than his fair share.

It no longer bothered her. After all, she'd put Dane in her past where he belonged years ago. Hadn't she? Standing here, within his all-too-compelling aura, she wondered if she was as certain about that as she'd thought.

'Not any more.' She took another long gulp to wash the sudden bitter taste of Luc's betrayal from her mouth.

'Oh?'

'There you are, Mari,' Phoebe interrupted with breathless haste, clutching her mobile to her breasts and saving Mariel from having to discuss her ruined career.

'Hi, Dane.' She barely spared him a glance, and Mariel had the fleeting thought that life had gone on here as usual while she'd been away. Phoebe leaned in and murmured, 'Kyle just rang. He wants to meet me. Now.'

Mariel stared at her sister, incredulous. 'And you agreed? What happened to your New Year's resolution?'

Phoebe bit her lip. 'I know, I know, but…'

'Don't let him call the shots, Pheebes.'

'I won't. But I've got to meet him halfway, don't I?'

Mariel raised a brow at the gleam in Phoebe's over-bright eyes. 'And where's that?'

'Um…a spot we like to go. Oh, and in case I don't see you, I won't be around when you get up. I'm on an early-morning flight to Melbourne. There's a music festival on. So I've asked Brad Johnston to drop you home. You remember Brad; he's keen to catch up with you again.'

'Ah…' Stomach sinking, she glanced over Phoebe's shoulder, saw the familiar fuzzy-haired guy weaving his way through the crowd. More than keen, if Mariel wasn't mistaken.

'You two came together?' Dane asked.

'Yeah, my wonderful sister came to keep me company…um…because Kyle couldn't make it. You don't mind, do you, Mari?'

'Of course not, but I think you should consider—'

'No need to bother Brad,' Dane cut in, his voice disturbingly deep, disturbingly close. 'It's all arranged, I'm taking Mariel home.'

CHAPTER TWO

'OH? OKAY...but...' Phoebe's eyes darted between the two of them.

'I'll let Brad know,' he told her.

'Okay. Thanks, Dane. See ya later, sis.' Phoebe pecked Mariel's cheek and was gone in a whirlwind of pink and perfume.

'*Arranged?*' Mariel muttered, glaring at him while every internal organ traded places.

'Wait here,' he ordered, and was gone before she could utter another word of protest.

Hardly. But she stood immobile, feet stapled to the floor, while she watched him dispatch Brad in less than five seconds. Why weren't her legs moving? Why wasn't she getting the heck away before it was too late?

Dane could tell Mariel was unsettled by the sudden turn of events as he made his way back. Her eyes glinted dangerously, that beautiful mouth a slash of coral in her pale face. But, he noted with satisfaction, she'd made no attempt to disappear amongst the guests.

'I was hoping to leave early,' she said the moment he reached her side. Setting her cup down, she unzipped the diamante bag that swung from her shoulder. 'About now, in fact. I wouldn't want to spoil the evening for you. You probably came with someone…' She pulled out her mobile. 'I'll call a cab.'

'I told you. I'm taking you home. And it's not a problem; I came alone.'

'Oh…' He saw her register that fact as her eyes clashed with his again.

Not a problem? Dane gave himself a mental slap on the forehead. They had unfinished business that went back ten years. To a night of youthful passion on a girly patterned quilt, the night-cooled fragrance wafting inside on the moonbeams.

Then a very ugly end outside his father's garage.

Not a matter that could be sorted out tonight, Dane knew, but he'd taken one look at Brad and some sort of proprietorial instinct had kicked in.

'But you'll want to stay, enjoy…' She waved a carefully manicured hand. 'Whatever…'

'I'm ready to leave when you are.'

'Very well,' she said with quiet formality, her spine rigid. 'Thank you. I'd like to leave now, if that's okay. My body clock's still on Greenwich Mean Time.'

'We'll say our goodbyes, then.' He placed a hand on the small of her back. He hadn't counted on the heat that rushed into his palm at that first electrifying contact. Beneath his palm the sensuous fabric of her designer dress shifted against her flesh, making him wonder how she would feel without the silk.

Just smooth, sleek skin.

She flinched as if burned. So she felt it, too, he mused as he steered her towards their hosts. Interesting. Had she and her French lover called it quits? She'd returned alone, and there'd been a definite chill in her reply when Paris had been mentioned.

The paparazzi, eager for their quota of celebrity guest snaps, were milling about the property's open gates. A security guard waved Dane through. Bulbs flashed and a blur of faces bumped up against the window.

'You'd be accustomed to this?' he asked, steering his way through the photographers. 'I should have asked if you were okay with it.'

'Yes and yes. But in this case they're not aimed at me.'

'That ain't necessarily so. You're somewhat of a celebrity yourself these days.'

'Not so much here. And it's not as if I'm your date or anything.'

He glanced her way before spinning the car onto the country road, leaving the press behind in a spray of dust. 'They don't know that.'

She didn't reply. In fact she looked serenely ahead, watching the moon-drenched paddocks and stands of gum trees flash by. Every so often a light glinted from a farmhouse behind the regular curtains of foliage.

She wasn't as calm as she let on, he noted. The grip on her bag was white-knuckled, and her thumbs massaged the strap in tiny jerky movements against her thighs.

Thighs that looked smooth and silky and...very naked.

Eyes on the road. Only on the road. Sweat broke out on his brow. He switched the air-conditioning to full blast. 'Too cold?' he asked a moment later, more to fill the silence than anything else. Silence that seemed to throb with the sound of the bass from the stereo speakers.

'No...no, it's...cool.'

She changed position, and he didn't have to look to know she'd stretched those long naked legs out in front of her. Within the Porsche's confines her roses-and-sin perfume wound around his senses like a long-forgotten dream. He thanked whatever lucky star was out tonight that it was only a short drive over the next ridge of hills.

Through childhood she'd always been his best mate, generous and loyal and stubborn. By seventeen she'd turned into a confident, ambitious young woman who wanted to take on the world. *And leave him behind.*

He shook off the edgy thought and glanced her way again. At twenty-seven... Well, right now she was all about lusciousness and impact. But how well did he know this grown-up version? 'You were saying you're not modelling now?' he prompted into the silence.

She hesitated. 'No. My business partner and I parted ways.'

'Luc?' She'd carefully avoided mentioning the fact that he'd also been her lover. 'Phoebe told me all about him.' Slight emphasis on 'all'.

'Yes. Luc. I don't want to talk about it. *Him.*' She waved a disconcerted hand. 'Any of it.'

'I'm sorry,' he said, and hoped he sounded sincere. And why wouldn't he be? He'd only ever wanted the best for Mariel.

'How's your father?' She spoke suddenly, as if she'd plucked something—anything—out of the ether to switch topics.

'He was okay when I spoke to him a couple of months ago.' And that was all Dane needed to know, all Mariel needed to know, and all he wanted to say about his old man.

'And your mother?'

'Still living in Queensland, last I heard.' With her man of the moment.

'So…by that I take it you don't live at home now?'

Home. Dane scowled at the white line dissecting the road as it curved over a rise. Had the generations-old homestead set amidst acres of rolling Adelaide hills ever been a home? 'Home' implied two parents who were committed to each other, their marriage and their offspring. At least it did in Dane's opinion; it seemed his parents thought differently.

'I moved out years ago. Soon after you left, in fact. I've got my own place in North Adelaide. It's close to work. Jus and I have an IT business there.'

'Then I'm taking you out of your way.'

'Not a problem. I like driving.' He glanced in the rear-vision mirror, frowned at the car which had been tailing them since they'd left the wedding, and with a sharp twist of the steering wheel pulled over to the edge of the road. 'Especially when you get a view like that.'

An almost full moon lifted out of the landscape, bleaching the fields and spilling inky shadows beneath the gums. From the corner of his eye Dane watched the car behind slow down, pass, then continue on.

'Oh…wow.' Mariel shimmied upright, her face animated in the soft glow. 'I've missed this. It must be the atmosphere here, but the Aussie moon looks so much bigger than the Parisian moon.' A quick grin danced over her features. 'And wouldn't they kill me back there for saying that?'

'They wouldn't if they were here,' Dane murmured, his thoughts tumbling back in time. As a kid, how many evenings had he spent watching possum shadows play amongst the trees against a star-studded sky? Gazing at the moon in all its phases?

Waiting until it felt safe enough to go inside?

He shook his head, edged back onto the empty road. Being with Mariel after all this time was tossing up old memories.

The last time he'd seen her she'd been careening down his father's driveway, grating gears and spraying gravel as she fishtailed onto the road.

He pressed his foot harder on the accelerator. The sooner he got her home, the better off he'd be.

The better off they'd both be.

A few moments later they approached her parents' home. Dane checked the road behind him again before turning into the driveway. Since Mariel didn't have a remote, he climbed out, punched in the code Mariel gave him on the panel set into the stone pillar and the tall gates swung open. They continued down a long drive, where blue agapanthus bordered a healthy lawn on one side, a row of old pines on the other. Ivy climbed the walls and iron lace framed a wide veranda. As they came to a stop three security lights winked on, but no light shone through the front door's stained glass.

He peered up at the blackened windows. 'Your parents out?'

'They left for a Pacific cruise yesterday. Thanks for the lift.' Her eyes flicked to his. He glimpsed nothing in those dark depths, as if she'd blanked all thought.

He didn't want her to go in yet. Not this way. Hell, not as this polite and distant stranger.

He reminded himself their childhood friendship had been years ago. She wasn't the young, innocent girl he remembered, with her fairytale dreams. She was a successful, mature and independent woman.

And what a woman she'd grown into. Those youthful curves had only grown lusher, and if it were possible her face more beautiful.

He switched off the ignition, sensed her instant panic. 'Mariel…'

'No.' She closed her eyes briefly. 'Not tonight.'

His hands tightened on the steering wheel momentarily. But tension showed in the lines around her mouth, the smudges beneath her eyes. 'I'll walk you to the door.'

'It's okay; this isn't the city,' she said, swinging the car door open.

'I'll walk you to the door,' he repeated, and pulled his key out of the ignition. Some things hadn't changed—still as stubborn as she'd always been.

And as fast—she was already halfway up the path before he'd climbed out. The aftermath of the day's heat still blanketed the earth, thick and smelling of dried eucalypt and pine.

Metal tinkled as she fumbled with house keys, holding them aloft and squinting at them under the porch light.

'Allow me.' Dane took the keys from her hands. The brush of skin against skin sent a tingle through every nerve-ending in his fingers, up his arm and straight to his groin.

The flash of awareness when their eyes met was a stark reminder that they could never go back to the easy camaraderie they'd once had.

He wasn't sure he even wanted that with her any more. Less than an hour in her company and his wants, his desires, were fanning to life inside him like a bushfire sweeping up from the valley floor.

She broke eye contact first, and a breathlessness caught at her throat when she said, 'Phoebe gave them to me, but I didn't ask her which one opened the front door…'

He fitted a key into the lock but the door opened without it. 'Not locked,' he said.

'Oh…that's probably my fault. I assumed the door automatically locked once closed.' Someone who didn't know her as well as he did wouldn't have noticed the slight sag in her posture.

Dane stepped past her and through the doorway, located the light switch. A warm glow from the antique foyer lights gleamed on polished wood and brass fittings, and brought a rich luxury to the burgundy carpet runner.

She glanced at the discreet panel on the wall as she followed him inside. 'Damn. I didn't even remember to set the alarm. Dad'll throw a fit if he finds out.'

'Only if you tell him.' Without looking at her, he started down the hall. 'I'll check the place before I leave.'

'That's not necessary,' she assured him quickly. A sudden nervous energy spiked her voice.

'Yes. It is. Anyone could have come in.'

'I look after myself these days.'

'I'm sure you do.'

A few moments later, ground floor covered, he started up the stairs, switching on lights as he checked the rooms. Mariel followed, muttering protests. He paused at the last door on the left.

Mariel's room.

So he left the light off. But as soon as he'd stepped inside he realised he'd made a mistake. Moonlight flooded the room, spilling over an open suitcase, a dressing table strewn with tubes and bottles. He breathed in the mix of feminine potions, powder and perfume like a man who'd gone too long without.

He'd never denied himself the pleasures to be found in a woman's bedroom, but at this moment he couldn't remember a single one that had ever compared to that one all-too-short time in Mariel's arms.

Dangerous thoughts. He dragged his attention back to the task he'd set himself. 'Everything seems to be okay, so—'

'Of course it is,' she snipped. 'I told you it was. But did you ever listen to me? No. Oh… Why did you have to come in and…? *Be you.*' She punctuated those final agonised words with a long slow breath.

The old guilt rolled nastily through his gut. In the pregnant silence that followed he heard the wind sigh through the trees, an echo of his own feelings. 'I thought that was what was so good about us,' he said, his eyes fixed on the moon but not seeing it. 'We could be ourselves.'

'Once upon a time, in a galaxy far, far away. Maybe.' Mariel switched on the light. He didn't know why, except that maybe the moonlit scene reminded her, too. He turned to face her. She'd folded her arms across her chest and was watching him with unnerving calm. Either that or she was a damn good actress.

'It's been a while, Queen Bee.'

He felt rather than saw her little hitch of breath at the use of her old nickname, then she pulled herself up straighter, lifted her chin. 'I'm not that inexperienced, trusting little girl any more.'

'*Dane…*' *Mariel said, reaching for him with passion-drenched eyes that hinted at vulnerability.*

The kiss.

Their first fully-fledged kiss.

A goodbye kiss, because she was leaving and for who knew how long?

He met her eyes squarely, ready to admit the pain he'd inflicted on her young pride an hour later. 'I was eighteen and an insensitive jerk.'

But that was then. This was now. And *now* was full of possibilities. She wasn't an innocent; she was an international sensation. A modern woman who'd no doubt had her share of men over the years—a thought he didn't particularly want to dwell on.

Her mouth twisted with grim humour. 'Has anything changed?'

A grin tugged at his mouth. 'Nope. Still that same insensitive jerk.' He couldn't help himself—he stepped closer, so their bodies almost touched, and brushed a finger down her cheek.

She shook her head. 'We're not those kids now. It's in the past. Leave it there.'

But Dane couldn't leave it there, whatever the hell *it* was, because his brain had ceased to compute anything so complicated as reason or words or sentence structure. All it recognised was the fragile face he suddenly found himself holding between his palms, emerald eyes swimmingly close, the seductive scent of her perfume, her hands against his chest and her indrawn breath as he leaned in to touch his lips to hers.

He tasted heat and sun-warmed honey, and he slid his hands through silky hair then down over smooth shoulders and chiffon to haul her closer, so he could absorb the fuller, richer flavour as her mouth opened for him.

He closed his eyes as her body grew pliant, melting against his. Fingertips scraping against his shirt. Soft throaty murmurs. Fast, warm breaths against his cheek—

Hard, flat palms pushing at his chest—

Heaving a breath, she reared back, eyes dark and wary. 'Why did you do that?' She touched the fingers of one hand to her lips then spun away.

Good question. Damn good question. He noticed the wisps of hair he'd dislodged from the clasp at the back of her head floating about her temples and around her neck. 'Perhaps I wanted to see if it was the same as I remember.'

She turned, eyes flashing with residual passion…or desire or anger—he couldn't tell through the sexual haze still blurring his vision. To give himself a moment he paced to the dressing table, picked up a bottle of perfume, set it down.

'And was it?' She closed her eyes, as if regretting the question, then shook her head. More silken hair tumbled over her shoulders. 'Don't answer that. I don't want to know.'

'Or maybe I just wanted to kiss you for old times' sake.'

He leaned nonchalantly against the dressing table as if his blood wasn't thudding through his body like a big bass drum. As if his jeans didn't feel as if they'd shrunk two sizes in the crotch. 'You kissed me back, Queen Bee.'

The shared knowledge singed the air between them, and she drew a shaky breath but didn't reply.

'And it felt good. You thought so, too.'

She let out a stream of air through her nostrils. 'Isn't that just a typically arrogant male response?'

'Am I not a typically arrogant male?'

She glared back, unsmiling, or was that a hint of humour at the corner of her mouth?

'Good,' he said, taking it as a yes and venturing a grin of sorts. 'Now we've got that sorted, I'll check outside.'

Mariel shot a hand up, palm out. Oh, no, she wasn't letting him off the hook that easily. 'Not sorted, Dane. Why don't we just get it out in the open now, then never speak of it again?'

His smile faded. 'Okay,' he said slowly. 'Why did you come to see me that night? We'd said our goodbyes at your place.'

'That kiss. It meant something to me. It meant *everything* to me.' Her heart twisted, remembering.

'It was a goodbye kiss,' he murmured.

'I thought—stupidly and naïvely, I realise now— that I was in love with you. And when you kissed me…like that…I thought…' She waved it away. 'Well, I went looking for you because I wanted to ask you…to tell you I was coming back…that we…'

That evening was still as clear as day in her mind. After *The Kiss*, she'd driven to his house. She'd seen his car lights on in the garage…

'I heard a noise,' she said. 'I was so pathetically dumb I thought you were in pain. Imagine my shock-horror when I saw Isobel on the bonnet of your car and you going at it like…well.'

She recalled that she must have made some sort of sound, because they'd both turned and seen her. Then bizarre fascination had held her in thrall for those few agonising seconds while her gaze swept the two of them and her heart shattered.

'I hate you, Dane Huntington, I never want to see you again!'

She didn't remember how she'd made it to the sanctuary of her car—it was the feminine giggle and the 'Poor Mariel' that stuck in her mind, and the sound of Dane's footsteps behind her, his calls for her to wait up. *Wait?*

Dane shook his head and she knew he, too, was remembering. 'Thing is, Mariel, as close as we were, as much as I cared for you, the one thing we never discussed was our sex lives.'

'Or lack of.' She held his gaze unapologetically.

'We should have. It would have saved any misunderstanding. I came by the next day to apologise, but you'd already left. So I'll apologise now. For hurting you.'

She nodded. 'Accepted. But you didn't have any reason to apologise. I realise that now. You didn't see me the way I saw you.'

Maybe not then. She read the message in his eyes and something fluttered inside her. Or perhaps it was something else that had stopped him.

'I tried contacting you several times,' he said. 'You wouldn't take my calls. You won't know I was in Paris a couple of years later. I dropped by to see you, but your landlady told me you were in London for the weekend with your boyfriend.'

'He wasn't my boyfriend; he was a fellow student.'

'Student, boyfriend—it makes no difference now.' He needed air. 'I'll go check the garden.'

It took a good ten minutes to scour the perimeter of the extensive grounds. Not that it was absolutely necessary. But it gave them both some time.

As he returned to the house light from the kitchen's stained glass windows flowed into the adjacent atrium, turning the abundant greenery within to the colours of amber and ripe plums.

From the other side of the glass he saw Mariel,

sitting on the edge of the raised pond beside a stone maiden pouring sparkling water from her jug. A moth, distracted by the light, fluttered above her head. Shards of crimson and gold light sliced through the fronds of a potted palm, danced on the water and reflected over the face he hadn't had the pleasure of looking at up close and personally in a long time.

She'd needed to chase her dreams overseas, he reflected. And she'd excelled. He'd been right in not taking their relationship to the next logical step. Thinking herself in love with him would have brought her nothing but grief. She might never have left, and he hadn't wanted to be responsible for that.

Marriage had never been on his agenda.

He focused on her once more. She'd braced her forearms on her thighs and held an open can of beer between her palms. Her posture drooped and he was hard pressed to remember any occasion when Mariel had allowed herself that indulgence since early high school. She probably hadn't noticed that her dress gaped at the front, revealing more creamy cleavage. Another tinny sat on the ledge beside her.

He took that as an invitation.

CHAPTER THREE

MARIEL tilted the can to her lips and rolled the familiar bitter Aussie brew around her tongue. So much for tonight's decision to avoid alcohol. The night seemed to call for it after all. She stiffened when she heard Dane's footfall on the marble tiles, then made a conscious effort to appear relaxed. Rolled her shoulders. Stretched her neck. Unclenched her fingers on the can. No way would she allow him to see the effect he'd had on her tonight.

'I didn't take you for a beer kind of girl,' he said, appearing from behind the foliage.

'When in Oz…' She tossed him the other can. 'Happy New Year, again.'

He caught it one-handed, popped the top, but remained standing a few steps away. It gave her another moment to take in the whole man. And what a man. He'd always had a well-toned body, but he was no longer the eighteen-year-old she remembered. He was twenty-eight and in his prime. His face had weathered somewhat under the harsh Australian sun, but it only increased his rugged appeal. Harsher jaw. Darker stubble. Eyes that saw more, knew more.

She forced away the shiver of disquiet that rippled

down her spine and looked further. Beneath his shirt he was all hard muscle. She knew because when she'd pushed him away earlier he'd been as unyielding as concrete.

Model looks? No, not smooth enough, not conventional enough, with that careless hair. Scowling, she tipped another mouthful of beer down her throat. He was more the dark heroic type.

Not hers.

'So what are your plans while you're here?' he asked, sitting beside her. He assumed the same sitting position as her on the edge of the circular pool, not quite touching her. But she could feel his body heat across the tiny space. Her skin prickled with the awareness that if either of them moved a millimetre she'd feel the hair on his arm brush against her skin.

She sat perfectly still and said, 'At the moment I'm not thinking beyond chilling out and surfing the sofa for a few days—*after* I've thoroughly reacquainted myself with my bed.'

And, yes, in the charged hiatus that followed she knew he'd caught the image she'd unthinkingly tossed out there. Damn.

He cleared his throat and said, 'You're staying a while, then?' into the charged stillness.

'Yes.' She had no choice. But she wasn't telling *him* that. He might still be Dane, but he was a man... The fiasco in Paris was still so raw and recent it brought a chill to her bones. Her shoulder muscles tensed and tightened.

'Mariel.'

She turned at his simple touch on her shoulder, ready to flee. Or fight. Or mash her mouth against his. *Sheesh.*

'I can feel the tension in your body from here.' He

set his beer aside and reached up, took a pin from her hair. 'For goodness' sake, woman, loosen up.'

She sucked in a breath. 'What are you doing?'

'When in Oz...' He took out another. 'I always liked your hair down,' he murmured. 'It'll relax you.'

'Relax...?' Her thoughts disintegrated. Mesmerised, she gazed at him, his eyes focused on the task as he concentrated on removing the clasp on top of her head.

'Yes...' Then his fingers were in her hair, and she was turning towards him while he loosened it, so that it tumbled down over her shoulders and released the pressure, massaging her scalp in slow circles on either side...

Oh, yeah... She forgot all about tension and tired muscles. She wanted to arch and purr and follow him to the ends of the earth. No one had hands like Dane. No one smelled quite like Dane. A hint of spicy soap and his own brand of musky, masculine scent.

And he felt right at home, with his body heat warming her all down her left side, while water trickled over the smooth stones beside them and the air was heavy with the scent of damp earth and vegetation.

What if she leaned in now and kissed him again? He was right: it had felt darn good. She'd watch his grey eyes turn smoky. She'd let her tongue slide over his, warm and decadently rich, like rum-flavoured chocolate...

And she'd be the one to pull back first, she thought darkly. Just when his mouth responded to hers. Payback time.

Or was it all too long ago to matter?

His hands dropped away. And maybe a corner of his mouth tipped up in a hint of a smile, maybe his eyes flickered with a one-step-ahead-of-you glint. Or maybe it was the barely veiled cynicism of a man all too experienced with women's ways. She couldn't be sure because she was still finding her way out of her little daydream.

'Goodnight, Queen Bee.' He rose, giving her an eyeful of male crotch. 'I'll lock up behind me. Pleasant dreams.'

Then he left.

As he should, Mariel told herself, pouring the rest of her beer into the fountain. Judging by the impressive bulge at the front of his jeans, one moment more might have been too late.

Pleasant dreams? Hours later Mariel lay on her bed, staring up at the familiar ceiling. Night air chased goosebumps over her naked body, pebbling her nipples and making the hairs on her arms stand up. The draught through the window was an uncomfortably warm northerly. But the heatwave conditions weren't the cause of her shivers.

Linen *shwupped* beneath her restless feet as she shifted for the zillionth time. Her lips still tingled from their encounter with Dane's; she could still smell his scent in her room.

She frowned into the dark. Despite her attempts to put tonight to the back of her mind, stubborn images— make that one stubborn image—refused to co-operate.

She'd first locked eyes with Dane when Justin had kissed her and tipped her off that he was there. She'd been subjected to that familiar cool and casual gaze he was so good at.

Ah, but at other moments his eyes had blowtorched her with such searing heat she'd wondered how her skin hadn't blistered.

It was still there between them, that connection, like the ghost of Christmases past. She'd thought she was over it; she'd even put it behind her and moved on with Luc, but had she been fooling herself all these years?

She'd come to Dane, her closest friend, looking for comfort and support on the eve of her first solo overseas adventure. He'd come upstairs to help her close her suitcase. Then, in a fit of nerves and excess energy, she'd decided to rearrange her furniture...

They shifted the shabby-chic dressing table she'd bought at a little French provincial shop in town, relocated her blanket box, then she'd flopped back on her bed.

She'd stared up at the ceiling and told him she'd paint it indigo, like the night sky. And that she'd paint gold stars and suspend a crescent moon over the mirror. If she was staying.

He'd watched her in silence, but her young heart had been sure...

She'd taken his hand and pulled him down onto the bed so that they were both staring up and sharing her sugarplum dreams. Then, in that typically female way, she'd succumbed to the tears she'd been fighting all day.

Yes, she wanted to study overseas. She wanted a career. But she was coming back. Because she had someone to come back to. Dane.

She just hadn't told him that.

She'd thought she was in love... And then they'd shared the most dreamy, most poignant kiss of all...

She shook the memories away. She was over it. Over him. Teenage heartache was always the most painful. The most memorable.

Years later she'd allowed herself to be swept away by another man. Flattered by his promises to make her a celebrity. Seduced by his smooth European looks, charm and attention. She'd thought she was in love again.

Just went to prove she couldn't trust her heart. From now on she'd make decisions with her head and leave emotion out of it.

She sighed into the darkness. Dane had changed, too. He was more remote, more cynical. More attractive. Just as she wasn't that starry-eyed girl any more, who'd spun impossible dreams around a moonlit night and a goodbye kiss.

Dane rolled over and picked up the bedside phone, checking the clock's digital readout as he did so. Seven a.m.

'Good morning, Mr Huntington.' A cheery male voice greeted him.

He leaned up on one elbow. 'Who is this, and how the hell did you get this number?'

'The name's Bronson; I'm a reporter with—'

'I don't care who you're with—'

'Is it true that your reunion with Ms Davenport last night has you rethinking your Bachelor of the Year status?'

What the…? He shot up, swung his legs over the side of the bed. 'No comment.' He slammed the phone back on its cradle.

So they hadn't wasted any time digging up the past, had they? Running both hands through his dishevelled hair, he peered through his upstairs window. The high security wall bordering his North Adelaide home kept intruders out.

Mariel. She was alone out there in her parents' house.

Damn. He needed to get out there ASAP.

Mariel didn't deserve to be dragged into the media circus his life had become since he'd been named Bachelor of the Year. His gut told him she was dealing with some heavy-duty stuff right now. Since he didn't have her mobile number, he punched in the Davenports' home number. It went through to the answering machine. Swearing a blue streak, he disconnected and headed for the bathroom.

Setting the showerhead to massage, he let the tepid water pummel his flesh while he cursed the day he'd allowed Justin to persuade him into what was rapidly becoming a *cirque des femmes*.

Teenage groupies who followed the Bachelor of the Year as if he were some kind of rock star rather than a respected businessman and charity patron. Babes from the magazine e-mailing him, contriving to bump into him outside his office, in the supermarket. He'd even had to give up training on his favourite running track along the River Torrens.

He was tired of the endless parade of women who'd manoeuvred their way into his life over the past few months, but he was Bachelor of the Year for another six months unless he made some kind of formal commitment with an eligible female, and that was never going to happen.

Unless... His thoughts turned to Mariel again as he poured on shampoo and lathered his hair. It didn't have to be a formal commitment... A regular date might just take the pressure off. A classy woman at his side. And Mariel was accustomed to the press. She had style and elegance and intelligence. Maybe they could come to some arrangement...

But did he want to get involved—in any way—with

the woman he'd never quite been able to get out of his system? He rinsed off his hair, reached for a towel. It was a moot point in any case. She'd never go for it.

Mariel woke to the musical warble of magpies outside her window. Pushing her hair off her face, she rose, reached for her robe. Last night's clothes lay in an untidy heap beside the bed. Not the way to treat her latest designer dress, which had cost her more than some people made in a year.

The knowledge that it might well be her last indulgence had her picking it up and slotting it into the wardrobe, before padding to the window and staring out at the bushland beyond the property.

The sun already had its claws into the day, scoring the rapidly drying undergrowth for any hint of remnant moisture. Heat and light. She stretched her arms open in welcome after the hibernation beneath heavy, restrictive clothing the European winter necessitated.

She rummaged through her partially unpacked suitcase. Fifty quick laps up and down the pool was just what she needed. Since she couldn't find her swimsuit, and she had the house to herself, she pulled out the first matching set of underwear she found: sapphire, with little cherries all over and a red satin trim.

At the edge of the pool she paused, then in a moment of madness decided skinny-dipping was the way to go and stripped off.

She plunged into the refreshing coolness and angled straight to the bottom, then up. As she sliced through its mirrored surface, she concentrated on the tang of chlorine, the pool's aquamarine lining and the burn of her muscles as she headed for the far end with long, slow strokes.

The last time she'd been swimming had been during a photo shoot on the Riviera in August, but she'd been working, and her enjoyment had been marred by the hordes of beachgoers and photographers. This morning she had the pool to herself. Pure luxury.

She knew almost before she surfaced that her notion had been premature. A ripple of sensation, as if someone had run their knuckles down the length of her spine, was her first and only warning.

Dane stood near the edge of the pool, a folded newspaper under one arm. Unlike last night's sinful black, today he was wearing white. Casual white shorts. White body-hugging T-shirt. Old. Worn. Soft. She imagined it against her fingers. Or her cheek. Her pulse tapped a wild, irregular rhythm. Unlike his top, his shorts were loose. They gave her a far too detailed and up-close view of tanned, hairy and very muscular legs. And, from her lowly position, more than enough exposed thigh...

She jerked her eyes to his. He'd slipped his sunglasses on top of his head and seemed to be rooted to the spot—

And then she remembered... Oh, God, she was stark staring naked.

She inhaled, gulping in a mouthful of chlorinated water, and managed, barely, to sputter, 'What are you doing here?' She glanced at her clothes and towel. Impossibly out of reach. Her cheeks filled with heat and the already irregular pulse picked up speed.

Stepping closer, to the very edge of the pool, he studied her with those piercing grey eyes. 'Watching you. Do you need rescuing?'

'No!' Oh, God. Oh, no. She sank as low as she could,

crossing her arms over her chest and struggling to stay afloat while every skin cell vibrated as if he was physically stroking her. The water was as clear as glass; no part of her was hidden from his powerful gaze. 'How long have you been here? Never mind. Pass me my clothes.'

'No need to panic; I've already seen you naked.' His mouth quirked and his eyes crinkled up at the corners. Lucky for her—or him—depending on one's point of view, right now they were focused on her face. But for how long?

The heat in her cheeks rushed to every tingling part of her body. 'Seven years old does *not* count. And I'm still traumatised by it.'

He picked up her underwear, held the items out over the water for her. Just a fraction too high, she knew— and he knew. She remained as she was.

'Wasn't my fault you forgot your towel and risked running bare-assed down the hallway.'

'Whatever you say. Hurry up.'

'Nice undies, by the way.'

She was acutely, devastatingly aware that he wasn't looking at her undies. A shiver rippled through her. The water suddenly felt chilled against her overheated flesh.

Just when she thought he wasn't going to play nice, he released them. They hit the water with a plop, floating on the surface just far enough away so that she had to uncross her arms and manoeuvre sideways a fraction. She snatched them to her with a murmured, 'Thank you. Now, if you'll be a gentleman and turn your back...'

'Thing is, Mariel, I'm no gentleman.'

For a few seconds the air hummed. The tension between them crackled. She couldn't reply, could only think that if she reached out she could wind her fingers around that calf and feel how hard that muscle really was. Then pull him closer and sink her teeth into that flesh. Fair punishment.

He took a step back, as if he'd anticipated such a move, then—finally—turned away. 'Did you realise there's a photographer a couple of hundred metres down the road?' His casual comment was followed up with an equally casual, 'They could have a long-range camera set up for all you know.'

Oh, hell. With shaking fingers she struggled to pull on the meagre covering—no easy feat underwater. 'Maybe they're just keen birdwatchers,' she said hopefully. Half decent at last, she hauled herself out of the water.

At the sound, he turned to her once more. 'You should be more aware of security when you're on your own. I could have been any stranger.' She snatched up her towel and blotted water from her face, bemoaning the fact that her complexion was winter-lily pale without its make-up mask.

'But you weren't. And you remembered the gate's security code—clever you.'

'Have you seen this morning's paper?' He tossed it on the little glass table between two loungers.

'No.' In a brisk flurry of movement she scrubbed the rough terry towel down one arm, then the other. 'Is it bad?'

'I'll let you decide.'

She felt his gaze on her and realised she was holding the towel in front of her as if she wasn't totally comfortable in her own skin. As if she wasn't used to men looking at her.

She wasn't used to *this* man looking at her.

His gaze drifted lazily down to her breasts, barely covered by her cherry-splashed blue bra, then lower, over the high-cut bikini briefs. 'If you don't watch out you'll burn that tender European-climate-accustomed skin.'

Burn? Her skin already felt singed and raw and tingling. Her nipples, already pebbled from the cool water, contracted painfully.

She swiped the towel over her body one last time, then swung it around her neck, fisted her hands and lifted her chin. Their eyes connected across the stone pool surround. 'So is it the society pages or the ghastly gossip column?'

'Check it out for yourself. Page twenty-three.'

There was a shot of the two of them leaving the wedding, and a smaller one of Dane's car parked in her parents' driveway.

> *The mystery woman on Dane Huntington's arm last night appears to be none other than Mariel Davenport, daughter of wealthy landowner Randolph Davenport, Europe's latest modelling sensation. Ms Davenport flew in from Paris and, it seems, straight into the arms of her old friend and flame. Could this cosy reunion signal the end of Adelaide's most popular Bachelor of the Year's reign?*

Bad. Bad. Bad. She didn't bother with the small print underneath. She tried to laugh, but the sound came out parched. 'Local gossip. You don't pay any heed to that rubbish, do you?'

His enigmatic expression didn't change. 'How do *you* feel about it?'

She shrugged and headed towards the house, the hot concrete burning the soles of her feet. 'It'll settle down in a day or two.' *When Dane resumes his regular playboy lifestyle.* 'I'm going to take a shower. Have you had breakfast?'

'I picked up croissants on the way, figured you'd want to share. They're in the kitchen when you're ready.'

She thought about the article while she took her shower. Being seen with Dane had cast her in a spotlight when she absolutely didn't need it. It wouldn't take much digging for someone keen enough to unearth the dirt on Paris and Luc and fling the mud at her. She'd never be able to set up a successful business here with that negative publicity. Hopefully the attention would fade when they realised there was *nothing going on.*

CHAPTER FOUR

DANE found coffee, a plunger and mugs, switched on the kettle and studied the business pages while he waited for Mariel to take a shower. He could hear the water running and schooled himself not to think about all that gorgeous flesh and warm soapy water.

Safer, much safer, to think about making that date he'd promised the robust blonde surfer chick he'd met in the bar last week. The fact that he'd had no intention of following up was irrelevant.

He looked up when Mariel appeared, and his gaze drifted over her of its own accord. She wore a navy mini sundress with a bright floral pattern and a white lace trim. It hugged that sensational figure and left miles of bare leg. Heaven help him.

'That feels much better,' she said, taking a seat opposite, her enticing still-damp fragrance wafting across the table.

He didn't agree. Ignoring his body's wayward but inevitable response, he poured them both a coffee, then, remembering, he withdrew a small plastic self-sealing bag from his pocket. 'I was cleaning out my car the other day and found Phoebe's diamond earring.'

'She lost her earring? In your car?'

He noticed Mariel's complexion fade, her green eyes taking on the hue of winter's frost-covered paddocks. Interesting.

'A couple of weeks ago, yes.'

She stared at him. 'You and Phoebe…?'

'Me and four women, actually. Drunk as skunks, talking dirty to me and giggling themselves silly.'

'Yeah, right.' She picked up her mug, but there was a smidgeon of uncertainty beneath the scorn.

'Ever tried to ferry a gaggle of women home from a hen night?'

'Hen night?'

'Amy's do. Drunk on Mai Tais, Screaming Orgasms and a male stripper. Well-endowed, too… Their words, not mine. The bride-to-be appointed me chauffeur for the evening.'

Mariel's expression didn't alter, but he saw something flicker in her eyes. She reached for a croissant, broke it open. 'I bet that put a dent in your social calendar.'

'Not at all.' He took a croissant himself. 'I'd do it for you if you asked.'

'Strip and ply me with Screaming Orgasms? No thanks.' She raised her mug, took a gulp, then set it down with a chink. Her crisp retort made him smile on the inside. But only for a pulse-beat, because the image she conjured with her sharp retort hit him right between the thighs.

He lifted his mug to his suddenly parched throat and took a long, slow swallow. 'I meant chauffeur duty. You don't have a car yet, do you?'

'Actually, I do. A pretty yellow hatchback. I'm picking it up today.'

He watched her eat in silence a moment, considering his words before speaking again, but he had to know for sure. 'What's the deal with your business partner?' He rolled his mug between his fingers. 'He isn't only your business partner, is he?'

'No. He—' She shook her head, pressed her lips together as if she was afraid of saying too much. 'And the word's *was*. He's history. Leave it at that.'

She drank her coffee greedily, then finished off her croissant in three quick, careless bites. 'It's handy you're here; you can put those chauffeuring skills to work and drive me to the car dealer. If you're not busy with any other…ah…commitments, that is.' Without looking at him she rose, carried the dishes to the sink.

'Clear schedule today.' And wasn't that handy? 'When do you want to leave?'

She rinsed the dishes, put them away. 'I'll be ready in a few moments.'

'That's what they all say.'

While he waited he finished off the business section of his newspaper. Twenty minutes later he folded it and wandered over to the window. What had happened between Mariel and her lover? He told himself it was none of his business. He was still pondering when he heard her footsteps cross the tiles.

She'd accessorised the sundress with hot-pink sandals and matching beads.

She looked fresh. Fun. Gorgeous.

His fists tightened in the pockets of his shorts. Once he'd have told her, but now, with this current friction like a live wire between them, it was probably wiser to keep the verbal admiration to a minimum lest it be misinterpreted.

She stared at him a moment, a small frown marring her forehead, as if disappointed to find him lacking in the compliments he'd have once voiced without thought.

Then she spotted his car keys on the kitchen table. Their eyes met and duelled in the familiar battle he'd all but forgotten. 'Uh-uh, I'm driving.' She got to them first, swept them up with a laugh and jingled them above her head. 'Your Porsche. All the way to town.'

'You think so?' He was behind her in a second, fingers tangling with hers, wrestling for possession.

Mariel's laugh snagged in her chest as his familiar deep voice vibrated against her ear and between her shoulderblades. The smell of healthy male sweat and Dane's own brand of scent seemed to wrap around her. She leaned back…or did he shuffle forward?…and his body bumped against hers and her grip on the keys faltered.

All movement ceased. Even her heart seemed to stop for one long breathless moment. His T-shirt shifted lightly against her bare back so that she was oh-so-aware of the hard abdominal ridges beneath. Over the whisper of the air-conditioning she heard the grandfather clock ticking in the hall. Felt Dane's hand locked over hers. The rough edge of a fingernail. His breath on her hair. The power he could wield over her, both body and mind… If she let him…

She hesitated a beat too long. She sucked in a breath, but it whooshed out again as he spun her round. She glimpsed the molten steel in his gaze before his lips clashed with hers. Hard, impatient. If she'd been able, she'd have used her hands to push him away but they were trapped between them. His heart pounded heavily against one palm; his car keys dug into her chest in the other.

She had no time to think as sensations battered at her. The heat of his hands on her bare back, her breasts flattened against his rock-solid chest, the sound of her pulse thundering in her ears.

As if he commanded it, her lips opened beneath his, softening and allowing his tongue entry, duelling with hers in an erotic battle of wills. His taste swirled through her mouth, the after-taste of coffee, and something darker, richer, smoother.

There was nothing gentle about it; this assault on the senses was nothing like last night's getting-reacquainted-and-see-how-we-like-it kiss.

It thrilled her. It terrified her. It gave her the strength she needed to push him away for the second time in as many days. She glared up at him, at the sharp angles of his face, harsh with a desire that had nothing to do with tenderness. Colour slashed his cheeks, his lips. She sucked in air, found it rich with his scent.

His eyes…she couldn't read them behind the storm she saw there. 'Who do you think you are, manhandling me that way?' she demanded, and was appalled at the breathy, *needy* sound of her voice.

'You're over him or you wouldn't have let me kiss you. Not last night. Not now. And definitely not like that.'

Like he really meant it.

Rather than tingly, her lips felt swollen and numb. She ran an experimental finger over them to check that they were still there. He'd told her last night that he'd enjoyed it, and that she had, too.

'Why did you come back, Mariel?'

'I told you, I—'

'Aside from catching up with family.'

She forced herself to take a slow, steadying breath. To take a mental step away from what had just happened here and focus on Dane's much more important question. 'I want to create my own fashion label, set up my own boutique.'

'You could have done that overseas.' His voice lost some of its hard edge. 'Or didn't you think Paris was big enough for the two of you?'

Because her legs barely supported her, she sank onto the nearest chair. 'It wasn't that.' She stared at her hands in her lap. He had to ask, didn't he? Better to get it over with.

He took a chair, turned it around and sat astride it, leaning his forearms on the back. 'Tell me.'

'Luc's a fashion photographer; smooth and sophisticated, and he swept an innocent girl like me away.'

At the low, throaty sound she looked up to see Dane's jaw knotted. He nodded brusquely. 'Go on.'

'He liked my designs, but he liked my face better so I modelled for him. We went into business together. The money rolled in, we got involved, I moved into his apartment. It never occurred to me not to trust him. But it turns out Luc's a drug dealer *and* he was having a fling on the side. I was just a useful addition to his cashflow. He was arrested on Christmas Day. I was taken in for questioning, too, and fingerprinted before being released.'

'The bastard.'

'Yes.' Remembered humiliation washed through her. 'My family knows nothing of this, and I want to keep it that way.'

'You have my word on that.'

The reassuring touch of his hand on hers threatened

to open the floodgate on unshed tears. And unwanted desire. She tugged her hand away, swiped at her eyes. 'So…anyway, I want to set up business here, but finances are a little tight right now.'

His brow lifted. 'I'd have thought you'd be laughing all the way to the… Don't tell me…'

'Yep. It's gone.' She rubbed at the tension in her neck. She felt like such a fool. 'And I'm afraid now my name's been in the press here—and linked with you—that they'll dig up the dirt I left behind.'

'Not if we give them something else to focus on and write about. Keep them interested in the here and now.'

'What do you mean?'

'We give them the impression we're a couple.'

'Couple?' she choked out.

'With eyes only for each other.'

A strangled noise escaped her throat. *As if.* 'There must be another way.'

'If you can think of one I'd like to hear it.'

Thing was, she couldn't—because her stunned mind was on overload, trying to process his outrageous idea. Still, maybe if they went on a few dates. Movies, theatre, a dinner or two…

'I need a regular companion to take some of the heat off this Bachelor of the Year thing,' he continued. 'Someone to accompany me to functions. It'll be good publicity for you, too, and if they do find anything about Paris my influence with the media here could come in handy. As for finance—I have an empty ground-floor room near my office that you can use rent-free to get your business started.'

She was still stuck on 'regular'. 'How regular are we talking?'

His eyes were like charcoal now, and intense. 'You'll move in with me—'

'Whoa. Hold it. *Move in with you?*'

'It's safer that way.'

'Safer for who?' Her gaze narrowed. 'And what's your definition of safe?'

'Your parents are away; you don't want to be up in that big house all by yourself. No one has to know what goes on behind closed doors, Mariel.'

Not an answer. Not an answer at all. 'So in the public's eyes we're a couple?'

'Lovers,' he corrected.

Heat spurted through her veins at the mental image. 'So we've gone from companion and a couple of dates to *lovers*?'

His gaze remained steady on hers. 'I won't pretend not to want you in my bed, Mariel.'

'What makes you think I'd want to be there?' she shot back.

What made her think she could resist?

'Vibes,' he said. 'Zings. Whatever you call them, they've been humming between us since last night. Can't say I'm happy about it. It complicates things.'

'For once we're in total agreement.'

'Problem is, we both want the same thing—but I'm the only one here willing to talk about it.'

Pressing her lips together to stop herself from giving in, she willed herself to look at him. Were his eyes a deeper colour?

'Your eyes are answer enough.' His gaze lowered to her breasts, which suddenly felt full and heavy. 'Then there's the way your body respon—'

'All right, stop right there.' She struggled to find air.

Why was there no air in here? Damn him for making her feel vulnerable.

For making her feel more alive than she had in years.

His expression didn't change, she noted with envy. How could he sit here so cool and casual and discuss the term 'lovers' and what amounted to a business arrangement in the same sentence?

She took another swift breath. It didn't matter; let him think what he liked about sleeping arrangements. Getting her business up and running was the most important thing right now. Good publicity and a place to set up. Forget vibes. And zings.

And if that meant living in Dane's house and masquerading as his lover... *An affair.* She swallowed... She'd bite the bullet and do it.

'Okay. Two sophisticated people like us should be able to pull it off without too many dramas. But this is a business arrangement. I'll pay you back once my business starts making money.'

She reminded herself he wasn't the type of man she dated. She loved glitz and glamour, and sophisticated men with a sense of style, whereas Dane still obviously didn't give a hang about appearances.

She needed to keep that in mind and put this unwanted, unhelpful attraction she had aside. For her career's sake.

For her sanity's sake.

As for Dane and his women... 'Though this is not in any sense a proper relationship, I do have a proviso.' She wanted to jump up and pace, but made herself sit still, lean back and meet his eyes. 'Men are very low on my priority list at the moment, so it won't be a problem on my part, but I won't tolerate any indiscretions from you while we're...together.'

'That goes without saying.'

'No. It doesn't. I won't be made a fool of again.'

'You've got it wrong, Mariel. The Frenchman was the fool.' Dane rose, returned the chair to its proper place and, with a gesture obviously aimed at taking her mind off her troubles, jangled the keys in front of her face.

'Oh...' Somehow he'd managed to steal them away. How had she allowed that to happen?

He opened her hand, dropped them in her palm. 'Let's go look at your new business premises and pick up this car of yours.'

Moments later Mariel ran her fingers over the Porsche's polished silver finish. 'Nice:'

'*Nice?* It's a 911 Carrera. A very expensive piece of precision machinery.'

'So am I, darling.' His eyes met hers over the bonnet and she wished she could unsay the flirty words which once would have brought a laugh to his lips. This time his lips didn't even begin to crack a smile.

She slid into the driver's seat, adjusted the mirrors while Dane made himself comfortable beside her—if sitting ramrod-straight *and* listing her way like a sinking ship could be termed comfortable.

'Relax, I'm not seventeen any more,' she reassured him.

'You've been driving in Europe for ten years. Don't forget which side of the road you're supposed to be on,' he told her. 'And remember, driving a car's like making love. You handle her gently.'

'Really?' She caressed the steering wheel a moment, studying him closely until he turned a quiet shade of pink. 'That's where I disagree with you. I'd say it's more about passion. Fast and furious.' She flashed him a quick grin and pressed her foot hard on the accelerator.

'What's the dress code for tomorrow night's do?' she asked ten minutes later as they coasted down the freeway towards the haze-covered city. 'Black tie? Formal?'

'Yes.'

'I'll need to buy a dress.'

His head was tilted back on the headrest, and his sunglasses hid his eyes, but she felt his gaze on her. 'Just keep in mind that I want to be able to slide my hands down your spine when we smooch on the dance floor.'

The way he said it—slow, sexy and appreciative—sent hot and cold shivers down her back. To make sure he didn't get the wrong idea, she said, 'To give everyone the impression we're a couple, right?'

He didn't answer.

She cleared her throat. 'Any further requests? Colour?'

'Surprise me. But make sure the zip glides easily. I wouldn't want to snag the fabric.'

Her pulse did a fast blip.

'When we get to town we'll organise a credit card for you,' he said. 'I'm guessing you'll want the whole deal: shoes, hair, etcetera. It's an important occasion for me, so don't skimp.'

'I never do.' Rather, she never had. 'So what's the evening about?'

'It's the year's major fund-raiser for a charity I founded a few years ago called OzRemote. This dinner and ball raises funds to support kids in the Outback with no access to computers or modern technology.'

'So you donate computers?'

'It's more involved than that. Money raised can pay

experts in the field to visit remote stations, instal equipment and offer technological support. I've got a trip coming up soon which will take me as far as the northwest corner of the state.'

'As I remember, Bachelor of the Year entrants have to raise a certain amount of money before they're eligible for judging and the "fun" part with the babes.'

'Correct.' He named a figure that had her nodding with approval.

'Impressive. I'll be sure to choose something appropriate to the occasion.'

The office space Dane was offering her was small, but Mariel focused on the positives. She had an address for her business when she eventually opened. Somewhere to store stock, spread out her designs and create in the meantime. She could renovate the little space at the front, dress up the window to attract customers. Employ her own tailor. Dreams, she thought. But they were *her* dreams, and Dane was going to help make them happen.

After he dropped her at the car dealer she collected her car, then drove back to her parents' home and packed her stuff to take to the city. She planned to spend the rest of the day on the all-important purchase of that evening gown.

Since this was an annual event, before leaving home she surfed the Internet for information on last year's ball. There she found a photograph of Dane and a prominent politician's daughter.

Blonde, big-breasted, statuesque. Naturally. Her full-length gown was an elegant sweep of crimson and the neckline dipped low. Very low. Dane's hand was curled around the woman's bare shoulder, hugging her close. Mariel ignored the little twinge. Her emotions were *not* going to become involved in this…*affair* they were embarking on.

It was late afternoon when she pulled up outside the address he'd given her in one of North Adelaide's leafy upscale streets and rang him to say she'd arrived. No pesky reporters that she could see as the high gates swung open.

She took a moment to admire the magnificent two-storey villa, with its bay window and its intricate detail in the veranda columns, stark white against the dark stonework of the nineteenth-century dwelling. A stone cherub cavorted in the midst of a circle of carefully tended low shrubs.

She manoeuvred her car into the empty spot beside Dane's Porsche and sat a moment, rolling her head back on the headrest. She was smart enough to know this arrangement couldn't lead anywhere. Dane wasn't her type, and he didn't do long-term relationships. But, oh, he only had to stand in the same room with her and her libido responded with a kind of sit-up-and-beg.

She didn't have time to ponder further because Dane appeared to help her unload her car. She followed him through a back door in the garage and around to the rear of the house.

Greenery and a variety of colourful flowering bushes filled an area enclosed by high stone walls. An in-ground pool mirrored the sky. A wall of glass doors, clearly a modern addition, opened onto the deck. He led her inside, through a kitchen boasting the latest appliances while retaining its old-world charm. They passed comfortable-looking dark leather couches and a vermilion rug on a polished blonde-wood floor. But it was the stunning chessboard on the coffee table that commanded her immediate attention.

'Oh, wow! This is magnificent.' She wandered over for a closer inspection.

'Black and white crystal. Handcrafted. One of a kind.'

Mariel picked up the king. It was comparable to a shampoo bottle in height, and like the other major pieces was tipped in gold. Dane flicked a switch on the side of the board, which was inlaid with mirrors and frosted glass, and the whole thing lit up from beneath. Another switch changed the colour of the light.

'That is one of the most magnificent boards I've ever seen.'

'I don't suppose you've learned to play?' he asked hopefully.

'You know me—couldn't sit still long enough.'

'Pity. Nothing I like better than a challenging game of chess.'

And obviously he didn't get the opportunity often, she thought, noting the fine layer of dust covering the entire thing. 'Your father taught you, didn't he?'

'One of the few lessons of any value that I learned from him.' His clipped, cold tone didn't invite further conversation on the matter.

Thoughtful, she set the piece down. It saddened her to think that after all these years there was obviously still bitterness between them. Not that she blamed Dane—it was just sad.

Upstairs, they passed an open doorway. 'Is this your home office?' Without waiting for an invitation, she wandered to the balcony. Adelaide's high-rise buildings jutted into an azure sky smeared with orange in the lowering sun, its reflection in the glass of the buildings flashing over the nearby golf course's casuarinas and pine trees. She breathed in the scents of summer foliage. Someone was cooking something Oriental; the fragrance of lemongrass and chilli wafted to her nose.

She turned to study the room. An over-crammed bookcase towered against one wall; an antique green lamp sat on the desk beside a modern computer. School trophies and a collection of model cars were displayed on another shelf.

'Come on, you can explore later.'

Dane opened another door and set her small rolling suitcase down. A breeze drifted through a partially open window.

Mariel saw a pair of French doors that opened onto the balcony, maroon drapes tied back with tassels, black lacquered furniture, a matching antique full-length oval mirror on a stand. The bed was covered in a quilt of the deepest merlot. He'd added a black throw and a couple of overstuffed turquoise cushions.

'There's air-conditioning if you prefer.'

'Fresh air's fine.'

'The bathroom's next door down the hall. You'll have it all to yourself; I had my own *en suite* built into the master bedroom.'

'Thanks.' She laid the day's purchases on the bed.

'Come down when you're ready and I'll fix us something for tea.'

As in they'd be dining in? With all these undercurrents swirling them into dangerous waters? She wanted, *needed*, to be amongst people. Lots of people. To go to the city and smell hot Adelaide pavement and hear familiar Aussie accents.

'Let's eat out,' she said. 'I know just the place.'

CHAPTER FIVE

THE SETTING sun had turned the sky gold. The city streets still held the day's heat. Tourists and locals strolled along North Terrace, past the lovely old railway building, now home to a casino and Hyatt hotel, where fairylights sparkled in trees. Others were enjoying drinks at open-air bars on the other side of the busy street.

From their little table Mariel glared at the spot where she and Dane had enjoyed many a meal—only the old pie cart wasn't there. A line of waiting taxis now filled the kerbside. 'But it was a more-than-century-old Adelaide icon,' she grumbled. 'I was going to shout you a pie floater for letting me drive…and for being a good sport about the close brush with the foliage…the very *soft*, very *overhanging* foliage.'

He tossed back a mouthful of beer. 'It's not really pie weather.'

'Any weather is pie floater weather, and I haven't tasted one in ten years.' She pursed her lips to suck lemonade through a straw. 'You know, I tried explaining it to Luc… How do you convince someone, especially a French someone, with vast gastronomic experience, that an upturned meat pie swimming in thick green pea soup and smothered with tomato sauce is a culinary delicacy? And has to be eaten standing at the kerbside, rubbing shoulders with cleaners to cops to politicians come rain or shine?'

He tipped back his glass, swallowed, then nodded. 'I guess you have to experience it.'

'Yeah...' She dropped her chin on an upturned palm and sucked on her straw some more, and for a moment they were kids again, shovelling pie and soup into their mouths, arguing over who had more sauce, waiting for the piecrust to turn sodden...

She didn't notice him move until the warmth of his hand touched hers. He slid his thumb over the inside of her wrist. 'So we'll make our own.'

The way he said that—as if he wasn't talking about pies, but something much more pleasurable. Her gaze darted to his and she found herself drawn unwillingly into the sensuous promise she saw there.

The guy watching her wasn't that teenager she'd known. Dane, the man, wouldn't hesitate to take what he wanted, be it in business or pleasure, and the knowledge shivered down her spine. She tried to tug her arm away, but his grip tightened.

'Don't,' he said, and lifted it to his lips, laying a line of kisses from the middle of her palm to her elbow, watching her with that heated gaze as he did so.

Sensation sparkled along her skin—much too brightly.

Her pulse beat a tattoo beneath his lips—much too loudly.

'We're meant to be lovers, remember?' The low timbre of his voice vibrated against her flesh.

Drawing a breath, she shook her head, as much to

clear it as to negate his words. 'No one's watching. You don't have to…do that.'

'Not true—you never know who's watching, and you should be as aware of that as I. Let's go home.'

'Dinner is served, *mademoiselle*.' Dane set the steaming, aromatic plates down on the French-polished dining room table. Two pies floated in a sea of pea-green, looking incongruous amidst the room's old-world elegance.

'*Ah, merci, garçon, c'est très magnifique.*' She smiled at him, a smile that reminded him of long-ago days, and said, 'But it's traditional to eat it standing.'

'To hell with tradition,' he said, pulling out a chair for her. He passed her a half-empty bottle of tomato sauce with the instruction to, 'Leave some for me.'

'You'll be lucky.'

Dane watched her up-end the bottle over her meal, then pass it to him. Only Mariel Davenport could eat a soggy pie dripping with red and green and maintain some modicum of elegance.

She sipped at her glass of wine. 'So your dad hasn't moved to the city?'

'No.' He stabbed his fork into the pie, hacked off a corner.

She frowned, censure in her eyes. 'I know it was bad for you as a kid. But he's old—he must be in his late seventies now. How does he manage on his own?'

'You know my father—he has a fit and healthy forty-year-old woman drop by to help him *manage*.' He chewed more vigorously, making his jaw ache.

'Oh.'

'Exactly.'

Mariel knew his circumstances. How both his

parents had indulged in extra-marital relationships. How his mother had left to live interstate with a new guy when Dane was seven. And how his father had paid for his only son to board at the exclusive school he and Mariel had attended because he didn't want the inconvenience of a son underfoot.

'I've done okay without his support,' he said into the silence. He'd worked his way through uni like any regular guy, waiting tables to pay his own way until he and Justin had set up their own business. It had exploded—way beyond their expectations. Five years, and financially he'd achieved what some would take a lifetime to do.

He didn't need family. Didn't need anyone. The women who flitted into his life either flitted right out again when they realised he wasn't there for the long haul, or understood where he was coming from and were happy with a temporary arrangement.

Wealth was happiness.

Strange, but tonight he didn't feel as happy about that as he'd thought. He set down his cutlery with a rattle of silver on china, reached for his wine, took a long, slow swallow.

'So I take it you've never changed your mind about settling down and having kids?'

Had she read his thoughts? His fingers tightened on his glass. 'You know me: terminal bachelor. As for kids—never in a million years. No way. No how.'

'That's sad, Dane. You're letting your own child-hood rule who you are now. There's nothing more precious than family. If you do want to talk about anything, at any time...' Mariel set her own cutlery to one side of the plate and met his eyes in the intimate lighting.

He nodded once. Mariel. Sincere, honest, caring. Soothing his mood the way she'd always done. The one person he'd always been able to count on. Unfortunately, right now he wanted her to soothe a lot more than his current mood. And with a lot more than words.

Forget it, Huntington.

Reining in his runaway libido, he straightened, flipping his linen napkin onto the table. 'I've got some fresh peaches, or a frozen—'

'Nothing more for me, thanks.' Patting her mouth on her own napkin, she rose. 'I'm going to be lazy and not help you with the clearing up. I haven't finished exploring yet.'

'Do you want coffee?'

'I'd rather have ice water, thanks.'

When he'd cleared the dishes, he found her in the adjoining family room, where she'd discovered his photographic equipment and was fiddling with his camera. She snapped his picture a few times in rapid succession, checked the results in the little screen. 'Definitely male model material. I didn't think so earlier, but I've changed my mind. I'll borrow this for a while,' she went on. 'Upload these pictures on your computer. Do you have a website?'

'No.' He set their glasses on the coffee table and began walking towards her.

'Not even for your business?'

He narrowed his eyes at her. 'You would *not* want to put those pictures on my business website.'

'You must be on a networking site?'

'Don't have time for gossip.'

'For socialising and sharing,' she corrected. She snapped him again, studied the image. 'There was a time when you used to share everything with me.' Her eyes met his, then cooled. 'Well, almost everything.'

Shadows of their youth swirled in those green depths, and for a moment he was lost in another time, another world. Shared hot fudge sundaes at the movies. Beach towels and barbecued sausages. The time she'd cheated on a test. The day he got his driver's licence and taken her for a spin in his father's BMW without his knowledge and put a ding in the passenger door...

He reached for the camera but she'd already whipped it behind her back. 'Getting slow in your old age,' she taunted.

'Or you're getting sneakier.' He closed the gap till their bodies were a handspan apart. Breathed in the scent of her honeysuckle shampoo.

'How do you mean?' She blinked up at him, all innocence.

He set his hands on her shoulders, felt the fragile bones beneath the smooth firm flesh. 'You know exactly what I mean. Using your eyes and the *you-used-to-share-everything-with-me* line as a distraction.'

As if the shoestring straps beneath his fingers weren't distraction enough. Not bra straps, he noted. Just dress straps...

Barely touching her, he slid his fingertips down her arms and felt tiny hairs on her skin rise as a shiver trembled through her. Imprisoning her against his body with one hand, he reached over her shoulders for the camera with the other, and down...

The reason for the clinch was forgotten. Everything was wiped clean from his mind except the sensation of her breasts snug against his chest and the fragrance of her skin. His free hand slid over the smooth flesh of her naked back, each vertebra in turn, as he slipped beneath the edge of her dress and the crisp fabric.

Her head tipped back and her lips were right there, smack bang against his throat. Warm, soft. Mind-numbing.

Anticipation tingled on his lips, danced on his tongue...

Damn.

This wasn't some nameless woman in a dark unfamiliar room where the slaking of lust was the only thing they had in common. He swore silently. Hell of a moment for his better self to show up. He wanted to throw back his head and howl.

Unlike last night or this afternoon, he knew he'd not stop this time until he had her writhing in pleasure beneath him. And she wasn't ready for that. Nor was he willing to take the risk with the ball happening tomorrow night.

So this time it was he who took a step back, kissed her lightly on those waiting lips with their sweet promise of passion and said, 'I've got some last-minute details to go over for tomorrow night; I'd best be getting on with them.'

She blinked at him as if she'd just woken up. 'Don't let me keep you.' Her husky voice dragged like barbs across his over-aroused senses.

'You might want to turn in early. Tomorrow night will be a long one.' He let the suggestion hang.

She nodded. Didn't say a word.

He turned away before he could change his mind, and climbed the stairs to his study. A man of his experience with the opposite sex knew when it was better to wait.

* * *

When Mariel came downstairs next morning Dane was already dressed. A suitcase and a suit bag sat by the kitchen table. He was standing at the breakfast bar, reading the newspaper and drinking coffee.

'Good morning.'

He looked up at her greeting, his brow puckering as if he was uncomfortable seeing her there. 'Good morning.'

He resumed skimming his paper, but she could feel the tension emanating from him like vibrating wire. 'Did I break a house rule or something?'

He flicked to the next page. 'No. Of course not.'

'What, then?'

He looked up again, met her gaze. 'I've never shared breakfast with a woman in this house; it caught me off guard.'

'You're kidding me. Dane Casanova Huntington has never had a sleepover?'

He studied the paper once more. 'I didn't say that.'

'So, what—they're the Cinderella kind?'

'I have a penthouse apartment in the city.' He tossed back his coffee, set his mug on the counter with a snap. 'I'm going to be busy all day, organising for this evening.' He stared through the window at the pool. 'I've booked a suite for us at the hotel, so I'll arrange a car to pick you up when you're ready to leave here.'

She was still processing the first bit. 'You keep a city apartment for *sex*?'

He exhaled slowly. 'I want to keep my private life exactly that. Private. I've also made appointments for a massage, spa treatment, hair and make-up,' he continued, as if she hadn't interrupted him with a question he obviously wasn't comfortable answering. 'Did I forget anything?'

She was still catching up. 'I don't think so,' she said slowly. 'I could do with a little pampering. Do all your partners get the star treatment?'

She saw nothing in his gaze, as if he'd deliberately blanked it. 'Tonight's important, Mariel.'

'I know that.'

'We'll be staying overnight, so if there's anything else you might need…'

Like her contraceptive pills? 'Overnight?'

'We want to give them something to speculate about. Isn't that what we agreed?'

Oh. 'Of course. The *press*.' The reason for this charade.

The press hadn't been the reason he'd kissed her yesterday.

Picking up his bag, he headed for the door, jingling his car keys. Impatiently or edgily? 'I'll join you in our suite at six-thirty.'

Mariel's entire afternoon session in the hotel's spa and beauty rooms were pure bliss. Courtesy of Dane, she was massaged and exfoliated, buffed and polished until her skin tingled, her complexion glowed, her hair shone and her nails sparkled. She had *The Best* in facial and hair treatments.

But beneath the pampering she couldn't stop thinking about this public affair she was rushing headlong into. She considered herself worldly enough to understand that mutual desire sometimes came without strings.

Except when it involved Dane.

She considered herself sensible enough to accept that it was possible to enjoy sexual intimacy without falling in love.

Except when it involved Dane.

And when a high-profile celebrity like Dane and she went their separate ways, as they inevitably would, she was going to have to live with the media attention for a long time.

She would *not* think about the other bad stuff she might have to learn to live with. Bad emotional stuff. Maybe she should make an advance booking for meditation or psychotherapy? She was likely to need it.

At six o'clock, in one of the suite's bedrooms, she stepped into her dress. A one-off European designer gown, it fitted so snugly it took a few moments to shimmy the silky white fabric up her body. As she tugged the zipper in the side seam closed the final wrinkles smoothed out.

But her nerves didn't. They tied knots in her stomach as she stepped into her sparkly stilettos, added a final touch to her upswept hairstyle and make-up. A delicate necklace of black diamonds flashed at her throat; a matching bracelet adorned her right arm. Her long platinum earrings swung as she studied her reflection side on.

Satisfied, she sorted her bag, then paced to the window to watch the late sunlight turn the River Torrens primrose.

She turned at the sound of the keycard being swiped in the door. Ridiculous to feel her heart pounding as if she was on her first date. She knew she looked fine, that this was exactly the type of gown his partners wore. Anyway, what did it matter what Dane—the king of dressing down—thought?

It mattered.

Taking a steadying breath, she turned. How did he manage to snatch her breath away every time? He wore black trousers and a made-to-measure white silk shirt that once again emphasised his shoulders and clung to his broad chest. His hair was still slightly damp and curled over the collar.

She fought the temptation to walk right on over there and smooth it with her fingers. To lean in and press her lips to that distracting V of tanned skin at his throat. Instead she kept her cool. 'No tie to a formal function—why do you ignore your own rules, Dane?'

'Because I can.'

Dane's answer was vague as his eyes swept down Mariel's body. God help him. How was he going to function tonight with that siren's temptation beside him? Because he suddenly seemed to have momentarily lost the power of speech, he motioned her to turn around with his fingers.

White. Floor-length. Skinny. Backless—below backless, in fact, revealing the lower indentation of her spine. Low scooped neckline that dipped...and kept on dipping. Which made him wonder how she kept the whole thing from sliding off her shoulders. A slit up one side that looked as if it had been created by an overzealous pirate's sword. He had to wonder if she wore panties at all...

'You want to talk rules?' he murmured, unable—unwilling—to tear his hungry eyes away. 'That dress is a rule-breaker. In fact, it should be illegal. One of your creations?'

Dismissing his suggestion with, 'I don't wear my own designs,' she whirled to face him again, the split in the fabric parting to show the long length of one leg. 'You think it's too much?'

'More like not enough.' He frowned, perplexed at his own reaction. He'd never been a conservative man, and enjoyed a good-looking woman as much as the next man.

'It's the latest Veronique design—*Sophisticated Style*. What's your problem?'

Problem? He'd always been more than happy to have the object of every man's desire on his arm. But was he *sophisticated* enough to make it through the evening knowing every guy would be falling over themselves to catch another eyeful of all that exposed skin? Because it was Mariel's skin. His own flesh tightened, tingled as heat simmered beneath its surface.

Weird. He didn't understand himself. On any other woman the gown would have looked stunning. *Did* look stunning. If tonight hadn't been so important, if he hadn't been the one who'd organised the event, he'd have called the whole thing off and suggested a night in. Just the two of them.

Fact was, he didn't want everyone ogling what he suddenly realised he wanted to ogle himself in the privacy of their own suite. What the hell was happening to him?

'Don't you have something…more? A wrap, perhaps?' *Blimey, just listen to yourself.* He needed to change his attitude fast if he wanted this evening to go smoothly.

Of course she looked lovely. Gorgeous. He'd be the envy of every man, and possibly every woman, in the room. And he intended to make sure everyone knew it was him she'd be with at the end of the evening.

Mariel stared at the grim-faced man before her. She knew she looked good, the dress wasn't vulgar, just sexy, so she refused to feel hurt or embarrassed or any of those vulnerable emotions. Temper was preferable, but it wouldn't be wise moments before they were due downstairs. 'No, I don't have a wrap. I don't need one.' She barely restrained herself from raising her voice. 'And, to use your own words, I'm going to wear this dress *because I can*. And I can—very well.' She snatched up her bag.

She had to pass him to get to the door, but a light hand on her arm stopped her.

'I apologise,' he said stiffly. 'You took me by surprise, that's all. You look sensational.'

Too little, too late, she thought, but she could try to be gracious—they had an entire evening in the public eye to get through. 'All right.' She let him curl her hand around his arm. 'We'll put it behind us and try to enjoy the evening.'

But how would the evening end, when the ball was over and an annoyed Cinderella retired to her suite with her suddenly stuffy prince?

CHAPTER SIX

MARIEL watched the floor numbers blink as the elevator descended. They stood apart, but their respective fragrances mingled, their breathing the only sound in a stilted silence until the doors opened and Dane took her hand and wrapped it around his arm once more.

The hotel lobby was alive with light and movement. Airline staff checking in, tourists heading out for the city's nightspots. Photographers snapping their arrival and that of other important guests, interviewing Dane about this evening's event and, as expected, their renewed acquaintance.

'What are your plans now, Ms Davenport?' asked a journalist, shoving a microphone in her face.

'I intend to start my own fashion label.'

'And your relationship with Mr Huntington?'

She met Dane's eyes and smiled coyly, allowed him to pull her a little closer and encircle her waist. *For the publicity.* 'We're just good friends.' Let the press put whatever slant on that they chose.

They passed a glorious Chihuly glass sculpture on their way down the pink marble staircase to the ballroom, where black mirrors on the ceiling reflected the glitter from crystal chandeliers, candlelight and a fortune in jewellery. An orchestra was playing light classical, and the scents of fresh flowers mingled with the latest French perfumes while several prominent politicians, including those holding the youth and education portfolios, mingled with society's elite.

Their table was the closest to the podium and filled with The Important People. She didn't feel up to any in-depth conversation tonight, and to Mariel's relief Justin's wife, Cass, was seated beside her, looking chic in a simple black halterneck gown, her chestnut-brown hair curling softly about her face.

'I've seen your photo in magazines, but it's exciting to finally meet you in person,' Cass said when Dane introduced them. 'And that's the most stunning dress I've ever seen.' She smiled ruefully. 'I wish I could get into something like that.'

'Thank you,' Mariel replied, unable to resist tossing a glance over her shoulder at Dane, who was standing behind her chair with Justin.

Leaning close, he ran his hand lightly over the nape of her neck and halfway down her spine and murmured, 'I think the challenge will be in the getting out of it.'

'I heard that, Dane Huntington,' Cass said, her eyes twinkling up at him.

As she was supposed to, Mariel knew. 'Indeed it will be,' she murmured back, then turned to Cass with a smile. 'So, you and Justin are recently married? I love weddings; tell me about yours.'

As Mariel had predicted, Dane moved away at the mention of nuptials and began conversing with a distinguished elderly man at their table. Justin sat down beside his wife and slung an arm around her shoulders, happy to join their conversation.

The food began arriving. Dane was busy between courses, introducing Mariel to people at the thirty or so tables skirting the dance floor. They ranged from colleagues in IT to contacts that might be useful to her in the fashion business. Everywhere he escorted her he made some sort of physical contact. A brush of his knuckles against her cheek, a finger-to-finger caress, a meaningful glance, a whispered word.

She couldn't say when the contact became more intimate. The glances hotter, the caresses more meaningful. Later, when he excused himself to talk business, she was aware that she knew where he was at any given moment. She'd look up and somehow there he'd be. And more often than not his gaze would meet hers. How long could you continue to play a game when the rules threatened to change?

During coffee he made an inspiring speech about the social, economic and technological disadvantages faced by people living in remote areas of the country, and how OzRemote was helping to address these issues.

Mariel couldn't take her eyes off him—along with every other woman there, she suspected. He was by far the most charismatic man in the room. He spoke with knowledge, passion and eloquence. She could understand why he wanted to shrug off the *Babe*'s Bachelor of the Year association; his respected business reputation didn't deserve it. He'd only participated in the contest to help raise funds for his charity.

'How long have you known Dane?' she asked Cass as they wandered back from the ladies' room later.

'Five years. I met him around the same time I met

Justin. They were just getting their business off the ground.'

Cass stopped, took a seat on a sofa, and Mariel joined her.

'I've never seen him look at any of his other dates the way he does you,' Cass said.

Mariel couldn't allow herself to think about that. She dismissed it with a half-laugh. 'That's because we've known each other for years. I'm not his usual type.'

'No. You're not a blondie, for a start. And he can't seem to leave you alone. This is the first time I've ever seen him look remotely serious about anyone since Sandy. But that crashed in a big way.'

Instantly curious, Mariel shifted closer. 'Who's Sandy?'

Cass lowered her voice and said, 'You didn't hear this from me, but Sandy was a woman Dane was dating a couple of years back. We all thought it might have been serious but then, as Justin tells it, Sandy tried to hurry things along by getting pregnant.'

Her words ricocheted through Mariel's body like a volley of bullets and lodged deep in her own womb. 'Dane has a *child*?'

Cass shook her head. 'Turned out she wasn't pregnant—just out to snare herself a rich husband. But he wasn't the happy father-to-be she expected. She changed her story quick, but it was too late.'

'She never understood him, then.'

Mariel understood. His childhood experiences were preventing him from taking the risk of making a family life of his own, and that, in her opinion, was incredibly sad.

The band struck up a lively nineties party tune as

they returned to their table, and couples took to the dance floor. Dane leaned close and said, 'My father's here. He's leaving in a moment, so we'll go say hello together. For appearances' sake.'

'Oh, Dane, he's supporting you here tonight? That's fantastic. Isn't it?' She looked up at him, but his face was a blank wall. At least his father had made an effort, she thought as he escorted her through the crowd.

'Mr Huntington.' She shook his hand, leaned in and dropped a quick kiss on his whiskered cheek. 'Lovely to see you again.'

'Mariel. And for God's sake call me Daniel.' His handshake was firm, the skin paper-thin. He smiled, and the heavy lines around his mouth deepened. 'Haven't seen you in years. This is Barbara.' He turned to the woman beside him, who was dressed in a low-necked frilly blouse and a long black skirt.

'Barbara. How do you do?' Mariel extended her hand and estimated 'Silicone Barbie' to be in her mid-forties.

Barbie's botoxed lips curved. 'It's nice to meet you.' Then her gaze rolled up to the stiff-necked man beside Mariel. 'Hello, Dane.'

He inclined his head. 'Barbara.'

'Oh, this is one of my favourite songs, and Daniel's not up to dancing tonight—just one dance, Dane?' she said, blinking her false eyelashes at him.

Dane could have refused, but he had a few things to say to his father's live-in lover. Now seemed as good a time as any. He turned to Mariel, let his lips linger on the sweet curve of her cheek. 'Excuse me, Queen Bee. This won't take long.'

'It's fine.' She waved him away. 'I'll keep your dad company.'

'I'm glad I've got you alone,' Barbara said the moment Daniel and Mariel were out of earshot. 'I wanted to explain about that night. The man you saw me with was my financial adviser.'

'Yeah.' Dane laughed without humour and leaned close so only she could hear. 'Since when did financial advice extend to a candle-lit rendezvous? A very intimate rendezvous, from where I was sitting.'

'I—'

'I'm glad you have a financial adviser, Barbara, because you're going to need one.' Not wanting to attract the nearby dancers' attention, he kept his voice low. 'You've wasted eight years of your life waiting for Dad to depart this world, because he's not going to leave you a cent. You're *not* going to get your greedy, *cheating* hands on the Huntington fortune.'

Her nostrils flared, her eyes widened and she tried to pull away, but Dane tightened his hold. 'He hasn't told you he lost everything he owned in the share market crash, has he? *I* bought the family property from him, to get him out of financial ruin. The home you're living in is *mine*. In fact, the dinner you just enjoyed was at *my* expense.'

The skin around her pumped-up lips turned white. 'You're lying.'

'Ask him.' Watching shock bleach the colour from her face was one of his life's more satisfying moments, and his smile was genuine as he escorted her back to her table. 'Thanks for the dance and the chance to talk, Barbara.'

Instantly she was forgotten as he turned to his partner for the evening. 'May I have the pleasure of this dance?'

Without waiting for an answer, he took Mariel's hand and led her to the dance floor. The band switched to a slow, romantic number and he came to a halt in the middle of the room, drew her close. So close that he could see tiny flecks of navy amongst the emerald in her amazing eyes.

He'd never noticed that before. He was discovering a lot of things about Mariel that he'd never noticed before. The tiny mole at the outer corner of her right eye. The way her eyes turned dark—midnight in a deep forest—when she was aroused.

They were dark now.

She stepped in closer, so he could no longer see her face, but her fingers stole up his shirt, the sides of his neck, then beneath his hair, where she stroked lightly with her fingernails.

The music throbbed in time with his heartbeat as his hands drifted over her bare back, absorbing the silken warmth of her skin, the fine hairs at the nape of her neck. She smelled like a fantasy of fresh flowers rather than of her black rose trademark perfume, and he nuzzled beneath her ear to inhale deeper.

'Dane…'

He thought she whispered his name. Like a sigh. But he couldn't be sure over the sound of the music. Did she make that soft sensuous sound when she made love? he wondered.

He could find out tonight.

Her cheek against his felt cool and soft, and his lips tingled as he turned his head slightly to taste.

He couldn't resist—he traced the graceful curve of her spine, down to where it arched against him. 'You were right. This is an excellent choice of gown,' he murmured.

'*I* thought so,' she murmured back, and he felt her cheek bunch against his as she smiled.

The music faded, or perhaps he just stopped hearing it. With his hand still on her back he pulled her closer, so that their bodies touched, breast to chest, thigh to thigh. She melted against him like butter on hot toast.

His body tightened, his pulse thrummed. He wanted to stay just this way, locked in this embrace, until the room was empty and they were alone.

But he was the host, and if he didn't pull away now he'd be an embarrassment to both of them.

He drew back and looked at her. Dark, *dark* eyes. Full lush lips that begged to be kissed. The pulse-point in her neck beat frantically, matching his own. 'I think that convinced them,' he muttered, a rueful smile pulling at his lips. 'It damn well convinced me.'

Her small smile took a while coming. 'Me, too.'

He escorted her back to their table, and then to give himself a moment to cool down excused himself and headed for the men's room. On his way back he saw his father, sitting alone on a sofa outside the ballroom.

He rose slowly as Dane approached, looking older than the last time he'd seen him a few months ago in the solicitor's office.

When Dane had purchased the family home so that his father could continue living there.

'Can we have a quiet word?' his father asked.

'What's on your mind?'

'I just wanted to tell you you've done a magnificent job here tonight. Thank you for inviting me and Barb to be a part of it.'

'You're welcome.' Dane's voice sounded brittle to his own ears. When his father didn't speak he asked, 'Was there something else?'

'Yes. There is,' he said slowly. 'And it's been a long

time coming. I haven't got many years left, and I've taken a good look at myself lately.' He glanced down at his feet, then looked up at Dane. 'It would have been easier to decline your invitation. Son.' He paused. 'Maybe we could let bygones be bygones and move on?'

Son. Dane wrestled with his emotions. It was the first time he could remember hearing his father acknowledge him as such. All those years when he'd wished his dad would toss him one crumb of affection. Dane had never wanted for money, privilege, social standing, but he'd have given it all away for family.

'Why now, Dad? Because I saved your ass? And you know that in the end I'm the only one who gives a damn? We both know Barbara's not going to stick around. I told her about the sale, Dad. It's time she knew.'

His father didn't answer. Just continued to watch him with tired eyes.

Despite all that had happened, deep down where it was only him and his maker, Dane yearned for the connection. But the past pain and the fear—yes, *fear*, dammit—of being hurt again was an impenetrable wall. Instead, he blocked all emotion and said, 'We've never been big on family; you're just getting sentimental in your old age.' He jutted his chin towards the woman he'd just noticed standing like an ice statue at the bottom of the marble staircase. 'Barbara's waiting.'

His father searched in his pocket for a handkerchief, then mopped his face. 'I'll be going, then. Goodnight.' He turned and began walking towards Barbara.

Shaken at his own callousness, Dane caught up, touched his father's shoulder. He was shocked at the frailty he felt beneath the shirt. 'If you need anything…'

His dad nodded without turning. 'I know.'

And as Dane watched him shuffle towards the stairs that lonely little boy inside him ached.

He'd never been so impatient for a night to end. With Mariel never far from his side, he discussed the upcoming trip north with those involved, made small talk with people he barely knew.

Outwardly he maintained his calm, professional façade, but anticipation sharpened his focus on the night ahead to a pinpoint. He couldn't wait to get Mariel alone upstairs.

Finally his hand tightened on Mariel's as the few remaining guests drifted out of the ballroom. They remained where they were while staff bustled in and out, glass and metal tinkling as they cleared tables, stacked chairs.

He looked at her. She looked back. Awareness glimmered in her eyes, desire softened her mouth. She drew a breath, drawing his attention momentarily to the amply displayed cleavage. But it wasn't only her body and the delights he knew that were awaiting his discovery that drew him to her and held him in thrall. It was the whole package.

Words were irrelevant. The whole evening had been building to this moment. Tension gripped him when their linked hands accidentally brushed his trousers. His kiss, when he leaned in, was restrained and chaste. He motioned to the door with their joined hands. 'Shall we?'

'Good idea.'

Still holding hands, they reached the door to their suite. He swiped the keycard and tugged her inside. City lights filtered through the window, casting an amber glow about the room. Even before the door clicked shut his lips were feasting on hers, and they went right on feasting as he whirled her around, pinning her against the wall. He didn't know where to put his hands first, so went with her shoulders. Smooth and fragile-boned. He barely lifted his lips to mutter, 'I can't be gentle, not tonight.'

'I never said I wanted gentle. Those were your words, not mine.' She laughed, a lightly hysterical sound. 'And you were referring to a car.'

She didn't object, and that was all he needed to know.

Tonight she was his, to pleasure and enjoy. The knowledge careened through his mind, through his limbs, as he gorged himself on her sweet honey taste. Like a crazed bee in a field of clover, he left her lips to sample every patch of bared skin, finally settling to suckle the tender spot between neck and shoulder.

Her fingers rushed up his shirt, popping buttons. Yanking the hem from his trousers, she spread the fabric wide to rub circles over his chest. The heat from her palms scorched and seduced, their impatience thrilled and tantalised.

There was no sound in their thick-panelled room save for the sounds they made themselves. It accentuated his harsh breaths, her desperate moans, fabric abrading fabric, skin rasping skin. The urgent sounds detonated small explosions inside him that reverberated like gunfire through his limbs. What they'd begun as a foil for the press had become something else entirely.

Or had they already known this was how it would be?

Impatience born of desires too long denied made his hands clumsy as he pushed the dress from her shoulders, leaving her breasts dazzlingly, breathtakingly exposed. Pale, creamy flesh. Dark, erect nipples.

Greedy now, he wanted more. He wanted all. He met her eyes, dark in the dimness. 'How does this creation come off?'

'Here.' She guided his fingers to the zip. 'It's tight.' He fumbled for a frustrating moment, then came the satisfying sound as it shirred downward. She helped him shimmy it over her hips. Her panties—if she was wearing any—went the same way as the dress. All she wore were sparkly stilettos.

Sweet heaven.

She reached out, flicked his belt buckle open, wrenched his zip down... In seconds he was as naked as she.

He toed off his shoes. His pulse was jack-hammering, his heart felt so huge, so tight, he thought it might be going into cardiac arrest. Was it possible to die of anticipation?

He twisted his fingers into her hair, pulling out pins, letting them drop wherever. Lifting her arms, she teased the silken mass out with her fingers so that it tumbled over her shoulders.

And then she was twining herself about him like a vine, gyrating her hips against his throbbing erection. She was all lean limbs and strong lines, and if his heart didn't give out he was probably going to spontaneously combust.

He'd never wanted like this, never burned this way. Tomorrow, that might concern him, but at this moment the only thing in his mind was their mutual goal. All the years till now, all the women till now, had been a dress rehearsal for this command performance.

Seemed he'd waited half a lifetime.

She'd waited a lifetime. Dane Huntington, teenage fantasy, here. With her. Mariel rubbed her lips over his, opened her mouth and drugged herself with his taste. Heat, desire, impatience. Dragging her towards oblivion. She couldn't think; her head was too filled with his scent. She could only feel. Sensations, lovely sensations, streaking over her skin and zapping through her body like golden lightning.

The ache low in her belly grew, expanded, until she was a writhing mass of wanton need. 'Now,' she demanded, arching her hips against his pulsing hardness. Instinctively she reached down between them.

His answering groan, harsh against her ear, had her shuddering. 'Protection?'

'On the Pill.'

He hefted her higher and her thighs wrapped around his waist. And he snapped, tension tearing free, his eyes smoking in the half-light, the hard planes of his body taut beneath her hands. No preliminaries—she didn't want them this time, didn't need them.

Still watching her, he shoved inside with one long thrust. They stared at each other for what seemed an endless moment, while needs and desire pulsed through their bodies and the air softened around them.

Then he withdrew a little, but only to push again, harder. Again. In a rhythm they both knew how to move to. He took, he possessed, and she met him hunger for hunger, greed for greed.

Her climax shot her into the realms of dark pleasure and bright chaos. She clung to him as he crested the wave and joined her in the sheer mindless joy of shared delight.

CHAPTER SEVEN

DANE was roused from sleep by a pounding on the door. Instantly awake, he grabbed one of the hotel's robes, stepped around last night's discarded clothing and padded to the suite's door.

Room Service with their requested breakfast. 'Good morning, sir.' The waitress smiled as he stood back to let her enter.

'Good morning.' He pushed a hand through his bedroom hair. 'It's nine o'clock already?' He'd slept like the dead. Hadn't slept like that since he didn't remember when. He did remember they'd finally found their way under the bedcovers together.

'Yes, sir. Five past, actually. We're running a little behind this morning.'

He found his wallet, dug out a tip while she set the tray on the table in the entertainment area. 'Thanks.'

'You're welcome. Have a nice day.'

'And you.'

Picking up the tray, he headed to the bedroom. Mariel blinked owlishly at him in the morning's golden light, then sat up, pulling the sheet modestly over her breasts and securing it firmly beneath her armpits.

'Good morning.' The words sounded formal and stilted to his own ears. He followed it up with a more congenial, 'I hope you're hungry.'

'Morning.'

Her hair was a wild dark halo around her face, and there was a glow in those cheeks this morning. He held himself personally responsible. But a thread of something approaching morning-after nerves wound through the satisfaction. He couldn't remember the last time he'd felt that way with a woman. Awkward. Clumsy with words.

Determined to banish it, he climbed onto the bed and set the tray between them, poured two coffees, handed her one. He figured they might both need it. He'd never felt the need nor the inclination for inane morning-after chit-chat. He either left a lover's bed before dawn or called her a taxi as soon as she woke.

'We slept in the same bed,' she said, surprising him. 'All night.' She didn't sound happy about it.

'There wasn't a lot of night left.' Thoughtful, he sipped the thick black brew. 'And, since there's only one bed, after we…' He drew back from the words. 'I figured you'd share.'

'A one-bedroom suite.' She added sugar, stirred. 'So…you *planned* this?'

Seduction 101: Never leave a woman feeling she's been taken advantage of.

He went with a smooth, 'Yes. I told you—the press want details.' He lifted the cover on a plate of fried eggs and bacon. 'We give them details—that was the plan we agreed on. Whether I slept here or on the daybed, the press will assume what we want them to assume.'

She sipped at her coffee. 'Okay. Fine.'

He was unsettled by this strange tension that had sprung up between them. He didn't understand her emotional tug of war. Last night she'd been molten lava in his hands. She wouldn't be thinking this was more than it was. Would she? She'd made it clear that after her Frenchman she wasn't going to get emotionally involved with anyone again.

'Why don't you tell me what the problem is?'

'There's no problem.' Her reply was quick, brisk, the tone casual. She smiled, but it didn't reach her eyes, and took another sip of coffee.

'We used to be able to be honest with each other—'

'Not completely.'

'Okay, you'll probably never forgive me for that, and I accept it. But I never deliberately lied to you. If we can't deal with issues that arise with our new relationship, then we *will* have a problem.'

She was silent a moment, and he thought she wasn't going to answer, but then she said, 'This is going to sound totally gauche, but I woke up and you were lying next to me naked and I don't know how to deal with this…us.' Colour bled into her cheeks and she looked down at the cup in her hands.

'Okay.' He took their cups, set them on the tray. 'I'll let you in on a secret. That makes two of us.'

'Really?'

She felt insecure. He heard it in her tone, saw it in her eyes as she darted a glance at him. 'Yes, really.' He tucked a finger under her chin. 'And don't look so surprised. I think the best thing now is to finish our breakfast, take a shower and head home. Maybe we both need some breathing space.'

'Good idea.' She took a token nibble of toast, then

dusted off her fingers in quick jerky movements. 'I think I'll just go and have that shower now.'

'Slow down.' He reached for her hand, lifted it to his lips and pressed a chaste kiss to the pulse racing at her wrist. 'Just slow down. You haven't tried your eggs. You were always crazy about cooked breakfast, if I remember correctly.'

She seemed to relax some, and managed a smile. 'And I remember you had an appetite big enough for both of us.'

He lowered her hand to the sheet. 'Still have.'

There was something dark, almost primal, in his gaze, and it had Mariel wondering whether he was still talking about food. A night's worth of stubble shadowed his jaw, and his untamed hair fell over his brow. Her heart started up the irregular beat that had become almost familiar over the past couple of days.

Clutching the sheet to her, she slid to the side of the bed. 'Good. Okay…' Her limbs went to water. She simply couldn't do sophisticated this morning—not with Dane watching her with those eyes. Eyes that soothed, yet excited. She even struggled with casual. Dane had seen every exposed inch of her last night, but in the light of day…

'I think I'll take this out onto the balcony,' he said, hefting the tray without giving her so much as a glance. Giving her privacy. Allowing her to keep her dignity. 'Nice view of the river from up here.'

She could have kissed him. No. *Erase that thought.* Before he changed his mind, she dashed naked to the wardrobe, grabbed her change of clothes and high-tailed it to the bathroom. Closed the door. Let out a ragged breath.

So much for her woman-of-the-world reputation.

She was immediately faced with her own reflection in the large mirror above the vanity. Sweet Lord, was that tousled woman with the thoroughly loved look really her? She stepped closer, staring at the wide eyes smudged with last night's mascara. The rest of her make-up had rubbed off hours ago. She explored her cheeks with her fingertips. Was that afterglow or whisker burn? *Emotion or lust?*

She whirled away and turned on the shower, waited for the room to steam up. Why couldn't she be as casual about last night as Dane? No mention of whether he'd enjoyed what they'd done—he'd been more interested in breakfast.

Not that she'd expected pretty words or a tender declaration of feelings. Not from a man like Dane. The truth was she didn't know what to expect from a serial playboy. After one short-lived relationship with a fellow Aussie she'd met while on a weekend in London, she'd only ever slept with Luc.

Dane's lifestyle was light-years from anything she'd ever experienced. She might have a glamorous career and international exposure, but he was still way out of her league. Nor did she believe for one moment his confession moments ago that he was still coming to terms with their altered relationship. He'd just said that to soothe her pride.

It hadn't, but it had been thoughtful of him to try.

She stepped into the black-tiled cubicle with its gold fittings and double showerhead to see if the soft spray could do the job instead. If she felt confused and somehow hollow and…dissatisfied, that was her problem, not his. She didn't know what he expected of her today or tonight. Tomorrow or even next week. Whether whatever he felt for her had changed in the past few hours.

Her head fell back against the tiles as the water caressed breasts still tender and tingly from last night. She only knew how he'd made her feel when he'd been inside her. Like nothing she'd ever felt before. Strong, fragile—a contradiction. It was too much.

It wasn't enough.

Desire—even overwhelming desire—could never be compared to love. And what Dane felt for her was desire.

But love… Love could make a fool of the most rational of people. It could tempt one to throw away every belief, every plan, every dream, and swallow you whole.

She should know.

She stepped out of the shower with renewed resolve. Love would never make a fool of her again. From now on it was logic and reason.

From the beginning of this arrangement it had been a tacit acknowledgement that they'd end up becoming lovers. It had been inevitable.

Just as it was inevitable that they'd end up going their separate ways.

They returned home together, then Mariel spent the next couple of hours at her new business premises a few moments' drive away. Not to avoid him, she told herself, but because it was vital to make a start.

The little room was bland, cramped and would need extensive renovations if she intended to use it for retail purposes. For now she concentrated on arranging the meagre furniture Dane had supplied, sorting through stock she'd brought with her from Paris and setting up her sketching easel. Since it was Sunday, she opened her laptop and made a list of potential suppliers and tailors to contact in the coming week.

Mid-afternoon, unable to concentrate, she gave up trying to work on her latest design and headed home again. She wanted to talk Dane into some photos of her work for advertising and display purposes. And it was time he was fully informed about her work.

She found him in the pool. He was stretched out on an inflatable raft, wearing brief black bathers and apparently asleep behind those sunglasses, because the only movement coming from the pool was the gentle lilt of the raft in the light swirl of air.

And, oh, my… She might have seen him naked last night, but it had been shadowed and frantic. She hadn't seen him like this, in full daylight. He was long and lean and liberally sprinkled with black masculine hair. The sun gods had hammered his skin to a burning bronze and spun streaks of fine gold through his unruly dark mane. Broad shoulders, six-pack abs, firm, flat abdomen…

She breathed in a lungful of searing heat and he must have heard it, because his head swivelled in her direction.

'Hi.' His deep voice rippled across the water. She still couldn't see his eyes, and wondered if he'd been awake and watching her the entire time she'd been staring like some infatuated schoolgirl.

She shifted inside her sticky blouse, laid her tote bag on a nearby lounger. 'Hi.'

Tossing his glasses onto the side of the pool, he

rolled off the raft and disappeared into the blue depths, then popped up again at the edge, hauled himself out.

Water sluiced off his practically naked body, leaving rivulets in the dips and hollows. Droplets snagged on his chest hair. She noticed because he was walking towards her, his shadow looming ahead of him on the cement. She took another breath and lifted her gaze.

Perhaps it was the sun's glare behind his head, but she saw nothing except that wicked grin. She recognised that look. She'd seen it too many times as a teenager to dismiss it. It stunned her that he could change from lover to friend just that casually.

'No.' She took a step back.

He grinned, revealing even white teeth. The crease in his right cheek. A black sense of humour.

She backed up another step. 'Don't be ridiculous. We're not kids…'

Grabbing her around the waist, he rubbed his wet body against hers and shook his hair, scattering drops.

She screamed, wriggling out of his grasp, her breasts grazing hard, muscled body. 'Not fair!' She glared down at her wet-splotched blouse, then at him, and grinned despite herself. For a moment—deliberately, she thought—he'd made her forget the morning's awkwardness. It calmed her, settled her. Almost. To her surprise, she found herself playing his game. 'You idiot—just look at me.'

'I am.' His voice dropped a notch, and his eyes turned from mischievous to molten, but he reached for a towel and rubbed it over his chest. The rasping sound reminded her of how that crisp masculine hair had felt last night, rubbing against her breasts. Her nipples tightened against her bra.

To divert his attention from her wet blouse, and to give herself a moment to steady, she yanked the towel from his hands and used it to swipe at her linen trousers. Then hunted a tissue from her pocket and dabbed moisture from her face and neck.

'Just for that, you can pour me a drink.' She sank onto the nearest recliner under a large green umbrella. A moment later ice chinked as he poured lemonade into tall glasses and set the pitcher back on the little ceramic table beside her.

He handed her the tumbler. 'How did you go?'

'Good. Thanks.'

He leaned down and moved in to touch his lips to hers, lingering. 'You should have let me come and help you.'

'You already helped, letting me have the room. And I didn't want the distraction,' she murmured against his mouth, while the fingers of one hand grazed the side of her face.

Dane was tempted to let his fingers drift lower. To unbutton her blouse. To unzip her trousers and make love to her here in the sunlight. Instead he drew back, planted a kiss on her nose and straightened.

He retrieved his sunglasses, slid them on, and sat on the other lounger, enjoying the sun's heat on his water-cooled body while he watched Mariel reclasp her hair on top of her head. The action pulled her blouse tight across her breasts.

He turned to study the sparkles dancing on the water's surface. She didn't know the outline of her filmy bra and two aroused nipples showed clearly through her damped-down blouse. He could smell her—a blend of make-up, perfume and sun-warmed skin. He also sensed her need for space right now. Closing his eyes, he made an effort to unwind.

'Dane?'

'Hmm?' His eyes snapped open to see a camera shoved near his face.

'Smile and look sexy.'

'What is it with you and photography nowadays?'

'It helps in my line of work.' She squinted up at the sun, then moved in, slid his sunglasses off his face, set them aside. 'Okay, go ahead and be surly. It only adds to the appeal. Women adore that look. You have perfect male model potential. If you'd just polish the rough edges a little.'

'I happen to like my rough edges. On second thought…' His gaze snagged hers and his attempts to unwind came to an abrupt halt. 'Depends on who's doing the polishing.'

'That would be me. Maybe a facial…' Leaning over, she caressed the side of his face with cool, slender fingers.

'A facial? Not in a million years.' But it felt so damn good he allowed her to continue. Maybe she didn't need as much breathing space as he'd thought.

She pushed his pool-damp hair off his brow, her lacquered nails doing incredible things to the front of his scalp. 'Definitely a haircut.' She aimed the camera again.

'I'm missing something here,' he muttered as she snapped off a few more pictures.

'Okay, I'll let you in on a little secret.' She checked the camera's images. 'I want some publicity shots for my work and I'd like to use you.'

'Me?' Incredulous, he slid upright. 'Me in a fashion catalogue, posing as some woman's accessory? That'll

be the day hell freezes over. Make that the day *after* hell freezes over.'

'No women. Just you.'

'Just me.' He squinted at her smile, frowned. 'What are you up to?'

'Okay. One of the reasons I wanted to work alone today was because I didn't want you to see my designs until I told you. I switched to designing men's fashion before I got involved in modelling.'

'*Men's* fashion? Why would a woman like you want to design men's clothing?'

'What do you mean, a woman like me?' Setting the camera aside, she sat down and looked at him with a kind of luminous excitement that made her eyes come alive. 'I happen to be very good at it. And I love the challenge. The preciseness, the detail, the perfection.'

Green eyes studied him, one perfectly arched eyebrow raised as she cast a disconcerting gaze from head to toe. 'Texture and style. I'm thinking of you in a steel-grey cashmere V-neck jumper. Something to show your shoulders to advantage.' She leaned forward. 'Will you?'

'Be your model? Not on your life.' He flopped back again to digest the new information.

She laughed lightly—an amused, tinkling sound. 'Sure you won't change your mind, Mr Eligible Bachelor of the Year?'

He slung an arm across his eyes because he didn't want to see the smirk playing around her mouth. 'I'm getting very weary of that line.'

'Why? Most guys would find it a hoot.'

'I'm not most guys. Frankly, I prefer to date women with more than half a brain in their head.'

'That's a sweepingly generalised statement. Not all the babes are blonde bimbos, surely?'

He raised his arm briefly, so he could see the smirk and give it back. 'You don't read the magazine. Obviously.' He paused. 'Besides, blondes are on hold for now.'

The atmosphere changed. He felt the sexual zing hum across the space between them.

'Okay,' he muttered. He might as well get it out of the way, because Mariel wasn't one to give up. 'What do you want me to do?'

'We'll take the formal shots here, then drive to Victor Harbor and do some more casual shots. Relax. It'll be fun.'

Fun? He could think of a lot better ways they could have enjoyed themselves this afternoon.

CHAPTER EIGHT

'I WANT your honest opinion.' Mariel selected a charcoal deep V-necked sweater from the pile of garments spread across his living room and held it up for Dane's inspection.

He ran a hand through his hair, feeling as out of place as a microchip in a blancmange. 'Nice?'

She shook her head in disbelief, her eyes twinkling with mirth. 'Too right it is. It's the finest quality cashmere. Feel it.'

She lifted it to his face, stroked it over his cheek. 'Light, yet warm.'

He'd never felt a more sensuous fabric. His imagination ran along the lines of how it would feel to lie with her on a rug made of the stuff and make love. 'And you want me to put it on. In thirty-five-degree heat.'

'Without a murmur of complaint.'

He scowled at the disarray. 'What else have you got lined up?'

'Relax, every piece here's casual. Except one.' She moved to a plastic suit bag, unzipped it to reveal a classic dinner suit.

'There's always got to be one,' he murmured, eyeing it with malice.

'Wait till you see the shirt…' She opened another bag, pulled it out.

'Let's get it over with it, then.'

Moments later he was staring at his reflection in a full-length mirror. He studied himself for several long seconds. It *looked* like an ordinary formal shirt, but… 'The front's transparent.'

'The *bib's* transparent,' she corrected. 'It's sheer, but not too sheer. Just enough to hint at all that gorgeous skin underneath…' Her gaze stroked down his torso like a hot silk glove. 'We'll set up in the front garden.'

Instant heat flooded his groin and he shifted his stance. 'If you look at me that way for much longer the picture will be unusable.'

She smiled, her luscious glossed lips full and inviting. 'Maybe I'm thinking I'll keep the picture for myself. As a memento.'

Smiling back and catching her hands in his, he leaned in, brushed his mouth over hers and murmured, 'Why keep a memento when you can have the real deal?'

As soon as the words were out, he realised why. She was one step ahead. Anticipating the day they'd go their separate ways. He fought the sensation that she was tearing him up on the inside. Permanence wasn't part of the deal. He liked his life fine the way it was. Had been. Would be again.

Backing up, he eased the tension in his fingers so he could let go of hers and cruise his hands up the slender columns of her arms.

'Dane…' She looked up at him. Desire still darkened her eyes, but the humour faded. 'Can we keep things light today? It's really important to me to get the business part of this right.'

'Sure.' He shook off conflicting emotions. 'Let's get this photo shoot out of the way so I can divest myself of this instrument of torture.'

Half an hour later, in his own jeans and T-shirt, Dane headed south along the coast with Mariel. They passed low rolling hills the colour of dried toast and a blue summer sea. The road, busy with tourists eager to reach the resort town, stretched out before them.

'Have you read the article in this morning's paper?'

'No time.' She reached for the paper at her feet, flicked through it until she came to the society pages and the photo of the two of them descending the stair-case that led to the ballroom.

'Well?' he said into the ensuing silence.

'"New Year's latest celebrity couple,"' she read aloud. '"How long will it be before our popular Bachelor of the Year steps down?"' He heard the slide of denim as she rubbed her knuckles over her thighs. 'It gives the impression we wanted.'

She read on in silence for a moment. 'Plenty of publicity for OzRemote. It says you're heading north in just over a week.' She folded the paper, set it at her feet.

'I arranged it around my work schedule. Justin's going to hold the fort. Come with me.' He didn't realise he had voiced the thought until he felt her gaze on him.

She paused, then said, 'No.' Another pause. 'This is your big moment. Our relationship shouldn't overshadow the great work you're doing. Besides,' she went on in a brighter tone, 'I'll be flat out with my own schedule.'

He reached out, touched her hand. 'Last night worked in your favour, too. You'll be a runaway success.'

'Speaking of last night…tell me about Barbara.'

'Barbara?' He shook his head. 'She's poison.'

'You two seemed to be having a heavy-duty conversation on the dance floor.'

'I said what I should have said years ago. She didn't take it well.'

'And that was…?'

'That she's a manipulative, deceitful bitch.'

'Strong words. How so?'

'I saw Barbara outside a restaurant several years back in a clinch with some other young guy, even though she's supposed to be devoted to my father.'

'Why didn't you warn him?'

'I tried. He accused me of interfering in his life and told me to stay the hell away.' His body tensed and his fingers tightened on the steering wheel. 'Haven't set foot on the property since.'

'He was talking about you while you were dancing. And I saw the two of you outside the ballroom later. There's regret there, Dane. And more.'

A tight ball of emotion rolled up from his chest and lodged in his throat. 'He made overtures about putting the past behind us.'

She touched his shoulder. 'Family, Dane. Forgiveness. Do you think you might be able to mend some bridges?'

He swallowed, forced the ache down and kept his eyes on the road. 'Do you think Adelaide's going to be rocked by an earthquake this afternoon?'

That evening Mariel sat cross-legged in one of Dane's big T-shirts in front of his main computer, uploading the day's pictures. As she scrolled through the images she couldn't stop anticipation trickling through her at the thought of what tonight might bring.

As long as she kept this arrangement strictly casual. Focused on the present. Took it a day at a time. They'd done okay today, she thought. He'd been attentive and considerate. Sweet, really. On the occasions he'd hugged her there'd been warmth and affection. Their interaction had been open and uncomplicated. Just as she'd asked him.

But the sensual promise in his eyes had been enough to keep her blood on a low simmer all day.

She glanced up, that simmer upping a few degrees as Dane sauntered into the room with a bowl in his hand. She snapped her eyes back to the computer screen and the task at hand. Ordered herself to focus. Plenty of good-quality shots to choose from. She was surprised at how well they'd turned out. Luc's photography skills had taught her something useful after all.

'Can I tempt you with ice-cream?'

'In a minute.' Her eyes didn't leave the screen, but her other senses instantly focused on the man behind her—she could multi-task, couldn't she? The velvet timbre of his voice caressing the nape of her neck. The heat of his body. His tangy soap smell.

The simmer heated to a rolling boil, and without thought she leaned back so she could rub her head against his abdomen. Absently, she tried to remember a time when she'd craved physical touch quite so intensely. 'This one.' She clicked the mouse for a closer look.

It was a shot of Dane in a dove-grey polo neck jumper with one foot braced on a rock, the turquoise ocean and white sea spray a magnificent backdrop. She'd taken the photo on a forty-five degree angle.

'Not bad.'

'Not bad? It's bloody brilliant. Okay…' She saved it to a folder she'd created, then clicked to the next shot. 'What were you saying about temptation? Wait…' She leaned forward, mesmerised at her own talent. Uncurled her feet and planted them on the floor. 'This one. Oh…yeah…'

In the picture Dane's arms were crossed and he was leaning against grey-brown weather-smoothed rocks on the seaward side of Granite Island. He was wearing a dark V-neck sweater over jeans and looking out to Antarctica. 'You do that brooding look like a professional model. Look out website, here he comes.' Even his long hair blowing in the constant wind that battered the island suited the image. 'You're okay with that? Being on my website? When I get one, that is.'

'We'll talk about it. Later.'

'Whatever, that one's a definite.' She saved it to her folder. Then squealed as a cold sticky tongue laved the side of her neck.

'Ice-cream.' He held a mouthful on a spoon in front of her lips.

'Is it honeycomb?' She darted her tongue out to taste.

'Is there any other kind?'

She closed her mouth over the spoon and let the cold creamy taste roll around on her tongue. When she'd savoured every last drop and licked her lips she said, 'I thought temptation was mentioned.'

'Ice-cream was mentioned.' His tongue laved her neck again, then his lips and teeth joined in, nipping and sucking her flesh. 'Is that not temptation enough?'

She closed her eyes and arched her neck for more, then moaned when a cold, moist tongue slid along her collarbone. 'It might be. It really depends on who's offering the ice-cream.' She could almost feel herself melting, sliding off the big leather chair and onto the floor. She gripped the edge of the desk. 'And what else they might be offering…'

She heard the clunk as he set the bowl beside the computer, and her body shivered in the delight of anticipation. His hands glided over her shoulders and then down. Inside the loose neck of the supersized T-shirt and over her breasts. Around her nipples in ever-decreasing circles until she was practically begging. Her head lolled back on the chair.

She heard the sound of tearing seams and the T-shirt's neckline disintegrated. In one quick movement he ripped the whole thing apart down the middle, leaving her naked but for her panties. Hot palms massaged her belly. Her head lolled forward and she saw her own body. The contrast of his hard, dark hands on her pale and practically quivering flesh.

Then she watched, breathless, as both his hands slipped beneath the flat band of purple lace over her hips. The erotic sight nearly tipped her over the edge.

A distant siren wailed. She was vaguely aware of the computer's hum, that someone along the street was playing party hits. Then she wasn't aware of anything much at all.

The muscles in her stomach tensed, then spasmed. Her arms fell away from the desk to hang limply at her sides. Her thighs fell apart as her feet skidded away on the polished floorboards.

Oh, dear heaven… How had she let herself become

so submissive so quickly? she wondered dimly. The little voice in her head warned her that allowing another man to take command of her in this way was a prelude to disaster. And, because this was Dane, he wasn't only taking her body—he was taking her heart. The heart she'd sworn no man would take again. But for the life of her she couldn't move, could only lie helpless and let him continue.

One large hand rose, tapped a couple of keys. The screensaver disappeared; an image of herself flashed onto the monitor. 'What do you see?' said the voice behind her.

She stared at the green unfocused eyes, the slack-jawed mouth, and managed to close it. Barely. She saw a woman who'd well and truly lost it.

She saw the glint of fear in the passion-dark depths of her gaze.

'Not me,' she whispered, shocked. As she watched the monitor she saw his face join hers as he bent down next to her. 'That woman is *not* me…' She tried to struggle up, but Dane's gaze was as captivating as any physical restraint.

'Yes,' he murmured. 'It is.'

His eyes smoked with intent as he parted her liquid heat with his fingers, then pushed inside, a long slide to paradise. His jaw chafed the place between shoulder and neck; his breath whispered over her breasts.

He withdrew slowly, circled the throbbing centre, then plunged inside again. Wherever he touched, heat followed. Pleasure. Hot endless waves rippled through her while the computer's inbuilt camera reflected it back.

Then she saw nothing but the bright sparkle of her climax as it carried her away.

The cheerful tones of Dane's mobile brought her back to reality with a jolt. The air stirred and his heat dissipated. He moved to the other end of his L-shaped desk to answer it.

'Hi, Jus,' she heard him say, as if he'd just been working over a particularly absorbing computer problem rather than her. 'No, nothing important.'

He chuckled, and her sparkle faded. Had he been referring to what they'd been doing? Biting her lips, she pulled the torn edges of the T-shirt together, clicked off the monitor so she couldn't see herself.

'I guess so.' The easy humour drained from his voice. 'What's so urgent?' He nodded, then a lopsided grin creased his face. 'In that case, how can I refuse?'

She heard him flicking through papers and stole a glance at him. He jotted something down, then said, 'Yeah. She's staying here for now.' He'd turned away from her as he spoke. He could have been talking about the weather. 'No…' His shoulders lifted, one hand fisted on the desk. 'That's the official line we're taking, yeah.' Silence while Justin spoke, then a low laugh. 'I don't think so.'

Did he already regret not being free to pursue whatever lady of the moment took his fancy? A shiver cooled the sparkling warmth she'd been enjoying just minutes ago.

She wanted him to look at her the way he'd been looking at her before. To show some indication that he'd enjoyed what they'd just done, that it wasn't all one-sided.

Her legs had recovered just enough to support her, so she rose and crossed to him, rolling the chair with her. He fumbled the pen as she inveigled her way between his body and the desk, but he managed to catch it mid-fall and jotted something else on his notepad.

His jaw was bristly when she ran her fingertips over it. 'What?' she mouthed, capturing his gaze with hers. His pupils swallowed up his irises until only a thin rim of molten silver remained. His confident business persona slipped. Whatever he had started saying to Justin slurred to a stop.

Finally she had his attention. She had Dane where she wanted him. Not Mariel his childhood friend, not Mariel who'd agreed to this arrangement for mutual benefit, but the sexual woman he'd made love to last night.

He shook his head. 'Can you repeat that, Jus?'

She'd ruffled that smooth exterior, distracted his ordered mind. She'd never felt such rush of feminine power before. It swam through her limbs like the most potent brandy until her head was dizzy with it.

High on the elixir, she smiled and prodded his chest, so that his body tipped back onto the chair. It rolled back a little.

'I'll…ah…need you to e-mail me that info tonight.'

On a wave of confidence she shrugged out of the tattered T-shirt and stood before him in nothing but her lace panties.

'When do we…um…when…?' His voice trailed away.

She slid her palms down her hips, stepped out of the last remnant of clothing, flung it over her shoulder. It landed on his desk with a quiet plop.

His eyes glazed over. 'No. Everything's fine. Just fine,' he choked out as she worked deft fingers over the front of his shorts.

Without breaking eye contact, Mariel took the phone from his hand—as easy as taking candy from a baby.

'Goodbye, Justin,' she said, and disconnected. She straddled Dane, satisfied she'd achieved her intended outcome. Oh, yes, she saw desperation and desire, both sharp as a sword and glittering in those grey depths.

'Right now…' she tugged down the zip, grasping his throbbing length with both hands '…I've a craving for more than ice-cream.'

Dane's brief chuckle turned ragged. His blood hammered through his groin, his ears, and every place between. 'So I noticed,' he muttered, before she crushed her lips to his and possessed him with fast, greedy bites. Long, luscious licks on fevered skin that cooled in the air as she feasted on his jaw, his neck, a shoulder.

She took him inside her with a cry that bounced off the walls and echoed like the thunder of horses' hooves in his ears. Conquest, triumph, victory. He saw it in the emerald fire in her eyes. He took her mouth and tasted it on her lips.

In turn, he possessed her with restless hands and frantic touches. Gave her what she wanted, took what she offered. Urgent, reckless, primitive.

There was no gentleness, no finesse. Just the frenzied race to the finish. And when it was over, and she collapsed against him, still it wasn't enough. He wanted more. He wanted to burrow beneath her skin, steal inside her mind. All. One.

Dangerous—this insatiable appetite. This all-consuming need. He enjoyed sex. But this sudden craziness was like an addiction that knew no limit. Which made him wonder: what the hell was it?

For one insane moment a couple of years back he'd even thought himself in love, but it hadn't lasted. It never lasted. The ability to love simply wasn't in his genes.

He drifted a hand over her hair, breathed her scent of sex and warm skin. He squeezed her nape so that she looked up at him with over-bright eyes.

'Wow,' she breathed. 'I'm good. I mean, I'm really, really good.'

The laugh that bubbled up from his throat was a mix of amusement and affection. 'Here I was, thinking it was me.'

Amusement and affection. He should have known with Mariel it would be that simple.

And that complicated.

His humour faded. 'I have to go in to work tomorrow.' He smoothed a thumb over Mariel's jaw.

'I thought you were on leave?'

'I was. But there's a problem with a computer system we installed a few weeks ago. Which means a quick trip to Mount Gambier.'

A day trip. 'And Justin can't go?'

'Jus and Cass are busy trying to make a baby, and it's Cass's fertile time, apparently. According to Cass's calculations tomorrow morning's the charm.'

Her eyes widened, incredulous. 'She's pinpointed it down to the hour? Are you for real?'

'That's what Jus told me.' The thought made him smile. 'What could I say?'

She grinned, too. 'Nothing but yes, I guess.' Her mouth softened, her eyes took on a sparkle, dew on spring leaves. 'Making a baby…'

Without warning the cunning image stole through his mind. Mariel, round with a child. With *his* child. He clenched his jaw against an unfamiliar crushing sensation in his upper chest.

He shook his head to clear the unsettling thoughts

that struck too close, too deep, and somehow messed with his perception that he had this situation with Mariel under control.

'That's convenient, then,' she went on, as if she hadn't noticed his silence. 'I want to work on some ideas, sketch a few designs. Acquire a tailor... I might even get some work done with you out of harm's way and unable to distract me.'

His brows rose. 'Me? Distract you? After what just happened here?'

'You only have to be in the same room to distract me, Dane. It's always been that way. But now I've discovered I do the same to you.'

His gaze drifted over her naked perfection. Already his body stirred with desire again. Fighting the irrational emotion that there was more to it, he shrugged and said, 'I guess we'll get it out of our systems eventually.'

Her delicate shoulders tensed. A weighty silence seemed to thicken the air. 'I darn well hope so.' Her voice was clipped as she climbed off him. She swiped her panties from the desk, shrugged into the remnants of his T-shirt and breezed towards the door.

He wished she'd turn so he could see her expression. 'I'll join you in a few moments.'

'Not a good idea.' She paused at the door. Only then did she face him, and her eyes were unreadable. Her compressed lips, however, told a story. She forced them into something approaching a smile when she saw him looking at them and said, 'We'd spend all night keeping each other awake and I'm totally knackered. Goodnight, Dane.'

He sat for a long time, staring at the darkened

doorway. He could hear her moving about in her room, could still smell her fragrance on the air. How the hell was he going to get back to normal without her when this was over?

CHAPTER NINE

MARIEL plopped face down onto her bed. She deserved an Academy Award for that performance, but she was pretty sure he'd bought it. Except for the fatal way she'd nibbled her lips. He'd seen it. Damn, he knew her too well.

Holding her pillow to her chest, she rolled over and stared up at the darkness. She'd managed to keep her tone as blasé as his. That was what it was all about, after all.

Her mouth twisted with grim humour. So she'd downplayed the intensity she knew they both felt by purposely bringing it up in conversation. He'd bought it, hadn't he? She needed to keep up the façade because that was what they'd agreed on.

Besides, she tried to tell herself, they'd never make it as a couple. They'd never see eye-to-eye on any damn thing—from personal appearance and TV shows to family and kids. Or commitment.

She also needed to make it clear they weren't going to do overnighters. If he saw her before she was wide awake she'd be vulnerable, and he'd see through her as easy as glass. It would be far too dangerous, because she was falling. Out-of-control falling.

Her heart seemed to curl in on itself; her fingers

clenched against her pillow. Time for honesty, she decided. She'd already fallen. Head over heels. Big-time. All the way. She was in love with Dane. Always had been.

Now she knew every intimate inch of his body, knew the sounds he made in passion, the feel of him deep inside her. Friends would never be enough, and 'lovers' was a temporary arrangement.

She sent her pillow sailing through the air, heard it slump heavily against the dark antique wardrobe.

But it was done now. And it was vital that she keep up the charade, that he never knew what she felt deep in her soul, because that would put him in an impossible situation. He didn't want permanency. He'd want to get back to his free lifestyle and bosomy blondes.

The bastard.

So she'd keep it light and easy. She'd make the most of the time they had and then…and then she'd walk away with the memories even if she walked away without her heart.

The following morning she kept to her plan. It wasn't as hard as she'd anticipated because Dane was in a hurry. He didn't stop for breakfast, grabbing a coffee on the run. But he did kiss her goodbye at the front door. A toe-curling kiss that went on and on and on, until the driver of the chauffeured limo waiting at the kerb to take Dane to the airport coughed discreetly.

Dane lifted his head and searched her face for a long moment. The early-morning sun struck his hair with gold, and heat blazed in his eyes, searing her cheeks. 'Tonight,' he promised.

She shook her head. 'You'll miss your flight.' It occurred to her then that they were saying goodbye as if they were a married couple, and she backed away, unsettled. 'Have a safe trip.'

'I'll call you.'

Blowing him a breezy kiss, she turned and walked back inside. Already she couldn't wait to see him again. To hear his voice again. To feel his body against hers again.

It felt odd, walking through his house alone. A reminder that she was here only because they'd agreed it was the best way. It was vital she keep those impatient wants in perspective, because she couldn't afford to want him this much.

If it were possible, their sexual relationship grew in intensity over the coming week. Because she wanted to work—and because she privately worried that they were becoming too close—Dane went about his business during the day and they only met up again in the evenings.

If he had a function to attend, she accompanied him. The press followed. They were a popular couple in the society pages. Speculation in the media mounted as to how long Dane would remain Bachelor of the Year, but he refused any interviews that involved talking about Mariel, insisting again that they were 'just good friends'. Nor did he give Mariel any indication that his status as bachelor might change.

They shared quiet evenings at home, took a moonlit walk on the beach late one evening after a particularly hot day, relaxed by the pool. Doing ordinary things couples did.

And every night, they came together with a passion that gave no indication of slowing down or fading. A love affair, she told herself.

And affairs ended.

But they cared about each other, respected each other. She refused to think beyond each day, determined to enjoy it while it lasted.

Mariel learned that Dane owned a string of buildings within the central business district. There were tenants to deal with, a minor plumbing emergency, renovations to approve. He made preparations for his upcoming Outback trip. It seemed he'd purposely filled his life with distractions to keep him busy.

And it bothered her that he'd turned his back on the only family he had. She lay in bed one night, staring at the ceiling, unable to sleep. She knew they'd had their problems in the past, but the remorse in his father's eyes on the night of the ball had convinced her there was hope, if only she could get Dane to see it.

Slipping out of bed, she grabbed her robe and padded downstairs. She poured herself a glass of milk, then carried it outside into the fragrant night air. Moonlight bathed the high stone walls and the luxury enclosed within. She turned to study the heritage building that was Dane's home.

Dane was a proud man, bordering on arrogant. Independent. Stubborn. Too damn stubborn to admit he might be as fallible as any other mere mortal. Everyone needed family, even Dane. She sensed that deep down he was a little boy, still yearning for that connection.

So he had women, acquaintances, business associates, but when things fell apart or tragedy struck, what then? If she could do one thing for him, it would be to try to reunite father and son.

'What are you doing out here?'

Startled out of her thoughts, she turned to see Dane standing in the doorway, a pair of loose boxers low on his hips. 'Thinking.' She walked towards him, pressed her head against his chest, listened to his heartbeat, strong and steady in her ear. 'Just thinking.'

'I can't sleep either.' His arms slid around her waist. They were silent a moment, while the crickets chirped around them and something rustled in the bushes.

Dane was relearning how to sense her moods, the way he had when they'd been younger, but tonight... What had brought her outside in the middle of the night? Had he upset her in some way? No. Mariel wasn't backwards in coming forwards. If she had a problem with him she'd let him know. So he laid his head against her bed-mussed hair and just held her.

She felt deeply, he thought, his hands wandering over the silken robe to absorb her body heat. Unlike the women who'd shared his bed over the years. Or perhaps he'd never known them long enough, or cared enough, to notice. No, that wasn't quite true. He'd had relationships that had lasted as long, if not longer, than this current relationship with Mariel. But this was different. Almost as if they'd become more than lovers.

No. He couldn't do that. Not to Mariel. He didn't want to hurt her. Would not hurt her. She meant too much, she was too important. Possibly the most important person in his life. He'd do anything to spare her the pain of falling for a man who couldn't commit. Which meant keeping to the same path they'd started out on. Smooth, level. Practical.

She shifted and relaxed against him. He squeezed her shoulders before taking her inside.

* * *

From behind the glass doors overlooking the pool Dane watched the low-slung canary-yellow sports car pull up under the carport beside his Porsche.

It was Sunday afternoon, the day before he was due to fly north. He'd be away for a week. Mariel had told him she had a surprise, and had made him promise to be home and not to argue with her when she got back.

The driver's door opened and he was treated to the mouth-watering sight of yellow stiletto sandals. As they touched the ground he noted that the sandals were attached to long shapely legs. No argument there. White-frosted toenails peeked out from beneath the straps and sparkly bits arched over her ankles.

Mariel climbed out, her dark hair tied back with a yellow ribbon. It looked as if she'd chosen the car to accessorise another neat little sundress, and it occurred to him that not many months ago maybe she would have.

He admired the shape of her bottom as she leaned over the back seat, then straightened with a box from the Chocolate Choices shop in her hands. Couldn't argue with that either.

She looked as delicate and deliciously cool as a slice of lemon meringue pie. Heat stirred deep in his loins and a primal growl rose up his throat.

Until the passenger door opened and his father climbed out.

The gut-punch knocked him back a step. Good God, what the hell was she doing? His body tensed as he watched Mariel walk with his father towards the door where Dane stood, hand frozen on the door catch. A ball of something thick and hard crawled up his throat. Straightening, he slid the door open before she reached it.

'Dane,' Mariel said before he could get a word out. Nerves flitted across her eyes. 'I've brought your dad to town. I know how much you both like chess and…thought you could get reacquainted over a game.'

His gaze swung from Mariel to his father. 'Dad.'

His father stopped an arm's length away. 'Hello, Dane. Mariel invited me, but if you want she'll drive me straight home again.'

Avoiding her gaze, Dane was tempted to tell her to do just that. He flexed his fingers. 'You're here now.'

There was anguish in his eyes, Dane knew, because there was empathy and understanding in Mariel's when he finally looked. He felt as if she'd stripped away his pride and confidence and left him naked.

He gestured stiffly to the sofa. 'What are you drinking these days?'

'I'll have a beer, if you've got one, thanks.'

Mariel switched on a CD. Light music filled the room. She slipped past Dane with an, 'Okay, then, I'll leave you two to—'

'Not so fast.' Dane grabbed her arm and practically frog-marched her to the adjacent kitchen. As soon as they were out of earshot he spun her to face him. Her eyes were moist. And angry.

She was angry? 'What the hell are you doing?' he demanded, his voice killingly low.

'I'm thinking about you, Dane.' She set her box of chocolate goodies on the counter. 'Your father needs you, and whether you know it or not you need him. I thought bringing him here for a friendly game of chess was a good starting point.'

He dropped her arm, strode to the fridge and pulled out two beers. 'I'd rather face a firing squad.'

'I might be able to arrange that.' He didn't need to look at her to feel her knife-edged gaze, as sharp as a slap. 'In fact, I might just perform the favour myself.'

His temper boiled over. 'You brought him here to play chess? Fine. You play. I'm not ready for this.'

Mariel hugged her arms around her body as he passed her, set the beer in front of his father and strode outside. The door slid shut with a thud that vibrated along the wall.

Ah, God. Had she made a really bad mistake? Her heart raced, her legs felt weak, but she made herself cross the room to face Daniel. Tension dug grooves in his already lined face. She'd upset not one person, but two people.

'He'll come round,' she murmured, then pulled her lips into a smile, pulled up a chair so that they both faced the chessboard. 'Meanwhile, why don't you explain the game to me?'

Daniel took three long gulps of beer then scrubbed a hand over his jaw. 'I should go.'

'Give him a few moments.' To distract Daniel, and settle herself, she picked up one of the beautiful black crystal pieces. 'What's this one called?'

Daniel exhaled a slow breath. 'It's a bishop. It can only move diagonally.' He picked up another. 'Whereas the knight can jump over any other chess pieces. The object of the game is to checkmate your opponent's king.'

'And what does that mean, exactly?'

'It's when—' He broke off when the door slid sharply open and Dane stepped back inside.

His expression gave nothing away. It was as if he'd

pulled on a mask. But he was calmer, Mariel noted. The tension in his shoulders had loosened; his hands weren't balled into fists any more. Some of her own tension ebbed. But only a little, because he was too cool. Too controlled.

He wasn't finished with her yet, she knew. She'd stepped way over the boundaries they'd set. She was his lover; that was all. Temporary at that. Which gave her no right to interfere in his personal decisions. Or his life.

Just because family meant everything to her, and she wanted one of her own some day, it didn't mean she had to inflict her lifestyle choices on anyone else. Not even Dane. Even if her motives had been purely for his benefit.

She sprang off the chair, nerves jangling. 'I've got things to do. Upstairs.'

Dane watched her go, then took the chair she'd vacated, set his empty beer bottle on the floor beside him. Outside, he'd been tempted to keep walking, to leave Mariel to clean up the mess she'd made. Until he'd realised she only had his interests at heart. Since when had anyone done anything like that for him? He quite simply couldn't remember. And he'd reacted like an angry schoolkid.

But he was a grown man, so he'd just have to suck it up and act like one. Didn't mean he was going to like it. 'Let's get it over with, then. White?'

His dad shook his head. 'We don't have to play.'

The beginnings of a smile tugged at the corner of Dane's mouth. 'You never did like to lose, as I recall.' He moved the clear crystal king's pawn two spaces.

His dad mirrored the move. 'I haven't played in years.'

'No excuses.' Dane made his second move. Queen, four spaces.

'Barbara left.'

'I know.' Both men studied the board. 'That's the kind of woman she is. I tried telling you that.'

'Women. You can't trust them.'

'Generally, I'd agree with you.'

'But Mariel's different, right?'

Dane felt his father's gaze on him. 'Mariel's not up for discussion.'

'Why not? She's living here. I read the papers. *Just good friends.*' His chuckle turned into a loud throat-clearing and he reached for his beer again.

Dane resisted the urge to defend their relationship. His father made it sound cheap. He studied the board but didn't see it. What they had could never be termed a cheap affair. He'd never known anyone like Mariel. Never would. The fact that he'd have to let her go at some point in the not-too-distant future suddenly loomed, and just for a heartbeat everything inside him stilled and nothingness yawned before him.

More rattled than he cared to admit, he pushed the thought away and made his next move.

Mariel remembered the chocolate cookies she'd intended offering them about ten minutes later. Chocolate always soothed troubled waters. She didn't want to interrupt or distract, so she'd put them on a plate, set it on the table and leave. She stole barefooted downstairs.

Male voices floated up the stairwell as she descended. 'You think you and Mariel might get—?'

'No.'

Mariel froze on the step at the categorical denial, fingers tightening on the smooth, worn banister.

'She wants to play happy families some day. Big old house, kids of her own.'

She'd always known he was going to end it, but to hear it spoken of in that detached and decisive way cut to her core like broken glass.

'Kids were never big in our family,' she heard Daniel say.

'We're not family,' Dane shot back. 'Being biologically related doesn't make a family.'

Well, at least Dane understood that much, Mariel thought. But she didn't want to hear any more. She climbed the stairs back to her room. Closed the door and lay down to wait for the afternoon to be over.

CHAPTER TEN

JUST on dark, Dane switched off the ignition. He had to admit it hadn't gone as badly with his father as he'd first thought. He climbed out of his car, but came to a halt at the garage door.

Mariel sat by the pool in the mellow circle of light. Right at home in the spotlight, he mused. Her long lashes rested on those fabulous cheekbones; her hair flowed over her shoulders in a stream of sable. At some point the sun had kissed the exposed skin of her shoulders and turned them rosy—strawberries and cream.

His mouth watered. One taste. Just one...

She'd probably still be mad with him. But she didn't look angry. She looked sexy. His blood heated at thinking about it, rolling and heaving through him like the restless summer thunder over the hills in the distance.

She moved, dipping her feet into the water, sending ripples across its smooth surface. A strange sensation hooked at his chest, snagging the breath in his throat and momentarily rooting him to the spot.

Growing up, she'd always been his port in a storm, keeper of his secrets. His best friend.

Now they were having an affair.

Nothing permanent, he reminded himself, watching her lean on her arms and tilt her head back so that her breasts thrust upward as if in invitation. A primal growl threatened to erupt, but he fought it down for another moment to watch her—she was so rarely still.

He walked towards her. 'Hi.'

Her head turned slowly towards him. 'So you've finally decided to come home.'

'I helped Dad fix a sticky door.'

Her lips softened into a smile. 'That's good. That's great.'

His bare feet made no sound as he crossed the pool surround. He stood a metre away, breathing her in, watching the rise and fall of her breasts, her nipples tight little buds against the buttercup fabric. Arousal, he knew. Just as he knew that if he bent down and touched the inside of her wrist he'd find her pulse as rapid.

'Shall I tell you what you're thinking?' he said.

She blinked once at him, but didn't answer right away. Finally she said, 'I'd rather you show me.' She tilted her head, and an echo of her thoughts lingered on her curved lips like honey.

The urge to drink that sweet temptation from her mouth consumed him. 'I thought you might still be mad. I take it from your response that you're not.'

'It's a waste of time holding on to anger, don't you think?' Dreamy emerald eyes stared up at him. 'I'd rather make love than war.'

He sat down on the deck beside her, picked up her hand, grazing his thumb over her fingers. 'Wise thoughts.' He brought her hand to his lips before setting it on her thigh and releasing her, then leaned back on his elbows.

His touch seemed to set off an explosion of energy.

She pushed up. Dane made to follow suit, but Mariel's bare foot in the middle of his chest prevented him. He could see her eyes clearly. Green and direct and aroused.

She wiggled her toes against his shirt. 'Make mad passionate love with me. Right here, right now.'

'Okay...' He admired the view of Mariel from this unique angle and said with a quirk, 'But it looks like you have the upper hand at this moment.' He scraped a fingernail under the erotic arch of her foot.

She jerked it away and let out a shuddering gasp as the first warm drops of rain speckled the deck. 'Damn you, that *tickles*.' Lifting her face to the sky, she flung her arms wide. 'Hey, it's raining.'

Her eyes clashed with his and she lurched as if drunk, except he knew she wasn't. His hands shot to her hips, as much to prevent her doing him an unspeakable injury as to steady her. 'I've got you.'

'Have you?' She crossed her arms and an unreadable expression crossed her eyes. He wasn't sure who'd manoeuvred what, or where, but he found her feet planted on either side of his torso. 'Maybe *I've* got *you*.'

He curled his fingers around her ankles. 'You sure about that?'

Anticipation filled the hiatus that followed, as if the evening, too, held its breath. He stared up at the clouds a moment, their heavy underbellies ruddy with the reflected city lights. Lightning flickered in the distance, followed by the restless grumble of thunder.

She glanced towards the darkening heavens, too. 'We should—'

'Yes. We should. Slowly this time. Very slowly.'

He tightened his grip on her ankles and looked into the smouldering depths of her eyes. They were dark, mirroring the approaching storm. Flicking her hair over her shoulders, she stared down at him, all glorious sparks and energy.

'Mariel...' Gazes locked, he trailed his hands up those smooth, firm calf muscles.

She didn't move or react in any way, but the pleasure of watching her eyes darken further with arousal while soft summer rain spangled her hair was like nothing he'd ever experienced. Though need pummelled at him, and urgency beat like a drum through his blood, his plan remained the same. Take. It. Slow.

Skin-warmed fabric slithered against the backs of his hands as he memorised the shape of her legs the way a blind man might learn Braille. The indentation behind her knees, the soft inner thigh.

She was silky heat and trembling need. His own fingers trembled when they brushed the damp cling of cotton at the juncture of her thighs. Anticipation, hunger. Both clawed at him as he slipped a finger beneath the flimsy barrier to find smooth female flesh. Slick. Wet. Hot...

For one paralysing moment Mariel felt her whole body go rigid. If the future of world peace had depended on it, she would have still remained where she was, eyes fused with Dane's while she absorbed the exquisite pleasure of his finger there. As if they'd never made love before, as if it was *different* this time. Chained by her own rampant desire, she was scared speechless. Motionless. Mindless.

Then his hand moved away, and *that* panicked her infinitely more. 'No. I—'

'It's okay, Queen Bee.'

'I know. I know it is.' She blew out a breath, pushed both hands through her dampening hair as she struggled against a tide that threatened to drown her. 'Now you're back, and I'm here, and it's slow and easy, and I'm still getting goosebumps. Because it's you.'

Feeling dazed, she looked down at the shoulders she'd slung her arms around in easy friendship, the familiar grey eyes she'd known since childhood. Except now those shoulders seemed impossibly broad and his eyes smoked with desire. 'It's been over a week and I still can't get my head around it.'

'Don't try. Don't think at all.' His tone was light as he touched his palms to the backs of her knees, but she sensed the tension hum through his body like a low electric current. 'Come down here.'

Easy, since her legs and every other body part were melting. Simple to slide, boneless, on top of him, to put her lips on his and drink him in. Slowly. He tasted of berries and beer, midnight and man.

She raised her head to stare at him in wonder. And amazement. Tangled her restless fingers in his over-long hair and pushed it off his face and behind his ears, breathing in the scent of his skin on the moisture-laden air. She lifted a hand to his eyelashes, caught a single crystal raindrop on her finger.

His fingers fumbled a moment behind her hair, then her zip was being lowered, baring her feverish skin to the refreshing rain. He was sliding the fabric away and she was lifting her arms and helping him, every movement, every shivery rasp of fabric against flesh, skin against skin, dreamlike in the softness of the night, until she was naked but for a scrap of ivory lace bikini.

He rolled her onto her back beside him and leaned up on one elbow. Backlit by the pool's underwater lights, his hair was haloed by a silvery rain mist. His gaze took a leisurely but scorching journey down her body—she could almost feel the moisture on her skin turning to steam, and barely stopped herself moaning.

'Yes. Now,' was all she could say.

He shook his head, his eyes glittering in the dusky dimness. 'You do everything at light-warp speed. Not tonight.'

He traced the side of her face with his knuckles, the barest touch.

And she forgot to breathe.

Forgot everything but the pleasure he promised.

Slow. He was true to his word. He cupped a breast in his palm, rolled the excruciatingly sensitive nipple between finger and thumb, then dipped his head to take it into his hot wet mouth and suckle, drawing the exquisite moment out like warm spun toffee. And again, as he paid the same loving attention to her other breast.

Languid. His palm, hot and heavy, was leaving her breasts to glide across her belly and down, slipping beneath the waistband of her panties.

Lazy. The long, liquid pull as he slid one finger over her moist centre. Deeper, until she moaned his name, the throaty murmur stirring from somewhere deep inside her.

Unable to help herself, she moved her legs and arched into his hand, restless, aching. Wanting. She'd never wanted this way with any other man. 'Dane...I—'

'Shh...' He rubbed his lips over hers, obliterating what she'd been about to say, then stared down at her. His face was part shadow, his hair haloed by the moisture's silvery mist, but his eyes… They were almost cool—unlike his kiss—and direct. 'Just lie there and be quiet.'

'But I—'

He kissed her again, drinking the words from her mouth slowly, the way he'd savour a rare vintage wine, until she couldn't remember a single one.

When he left her lips to nibble his way down the column of her throat and over the pounding pulse in her neck, she couldn't breathe. When he shifted and his tongue delved into her belly button, she couldn't move. When he laved his way slowly and sinuously over her abdomen to the edge of her bikini, she couldn't think…

He was smoothing the cling of lace away, the arousing ridge of callus at the base of his fingers chafing her skin as his hand slid down her thighs, over her calves until he'd divested her of the last shred of clothing.

And, oh… Ah… Yes… His mouth was hot heaven on her air-cooled flesh as he parted her legs and worshipped the swollen knot of need with his tongue. Hands alternately fluttering and fisting in Dane's hair, she floated somewhere between paradise and dawn.

The murky atmosphere dewed her skin with sweat and rain while a restless sky flickered and rumbled. Pressure, thick and white-hot, building, burning. Rising on a cumulonimbus crescendo that echoed within her.

She arched against him, the torrid shock of climax shuddering through her, a primitive sound issuing from her throat, tearing the sultry air.

But he didn't give her time to come down. Before she could draw breath he was plunging a finger inside while his mouth continued to suckle, relentlessly pushing her further, faster, higher. Gasping, she slid over the hot and slippery edge again. She closed her eyes on a moan.

Slowly she became aware that the plush-prickly sensation on her belly must be Dane's chin. She opened her eyes again and met his over the pale expanse of naked flesh. 'Oh. Wow.' Her lungs couldn't seem to find any oxygen, and she seemed to be incapable of muttering more than one word at a time.

'My sentiments exactly.' His voice was thick as he reared up, flicking open his belt buckle.

She laughed raggedly, struggling for breath as she wiggled down, beneath his body, until she felt the rasp of denim and the hot swell of his erection against her sensitised flesh. Buttons popped as she leaned up, tore open his shirt and rubbed greedy hands over hard, hairy flesh.

He snagged her fingers. 'Slow, remember?'

'Okay. But make it quick.' Slow had never been in her vocabulary. But she lay back while he yanked off his almost buttonless shirt, tossed it aside. He stood to shuck off his jeans and jocks.

And… She'd seen him naked, but it had always been in a fevered rush. Now… What could one say about perfection? Every feminine cell rolled around and lay down and begged at that magnificent display of aroused masculinity, and her pulse, which had almost steadied, picked up again at double time.

Dane. In the flesh. Glorious, touchable, within reachable flesh.

He lowered himself to the deck in one deft manoeuvre that swept what little breath she had left from her lungs, rolled her beneath him, almost crushing her in the process.

'Some women like to be smothered,' Mariel murmured, struggling for air and space. 'I'm not one of them.'

'Quit complaining.' But he took some of his weight on his elbows and stretched out over her, the lines of his body like some sleek and muscular predator. The hard length of his erection prodded against her pelvis. His chest rubbed up against her breasts as he coaxed her with light, flirty kisses over her face, her neck, her ear, where he whispered, 'We'll discuss personal preferences another time.'

He pressed his lips to hers, the kiss turning from playful to passionate in less time than it took for Mariel to form a response. Streams of sensation flowed over her skin as his fingers traced her brow, her cheeks, her jaw. His tongue delved inside, coaxing hers to join in with a sensuality she couldn't resist.

Reaching down between their bodies, she wrapped her fingers around him. He jerked in her hands, stopped kissing her to pull back and stare into her eyes. They remained that way for an eternity, gazes locked as she slid her fingers slowly from silky tip to throbbing base, then back to the tip once more. She smoothed the drop of moisture she discovered there with her finger before guiding him between her thighs.

No words. In the deep well of midnight, with the one person who knew her almost better than she knew herself, speech was unnecessary. Time was irrelevant. Their eyes met in accord. She understood him, his vulnerabilities, his fears, his needs. Just as she knew he understood hers.

The rain had almost stopped, leaving only the pungent smell of freshly damp vegetation and the remnant moist heat from the day. She heard the rhythmic *plop* as water rolled off a broad-leaved plant nearby. A patch of sky peeked through the clouds, its silver-gilded edge lit by an invisible moon.

A different kind of heat seduced her now, as he pushed his blunt satin tip inside her. A slow, delicious friction stroked and rubbed her inner muscles. A moan escaped her. The long, liquid glide to paradise.

Urgency grew, need sharpened as he urged her higher. She followed, and with fingers, lips, teeth and tongue she urged him, also, to pursue her.

She met him stroke for stroke, matching demand for demand, as their bodies moved in a choreographed dance. Like a perfect storm, he whipped them away together on a flood of sensation until they washed up on some distant shore.

Dane groaned—maybe she did, too; she couldn't be sure—and collapsed on top of her. Their eyes fused on the other's, lips close, breath mingling. His heart was drubbing like a piston against her own.

When he made to pull away, take some of his weight off her, she yanked him back with what remaining strength she had. 'Don't go.'

'I wasn't leaving.'

His silky hair brushed her skin as he smiled at her in the dimness. 'I was thinking we should go inside and find somewhere more comfortable. Maybe get some sleep.'

'Okay.'

Pushing up, he swept her into his arms and headed for the door. She clung to his neck as he climbed the stairs, barely raising a puff. And just this once she was content to let him play hero.

The cool, smooth sheets beneath her body lulled her towards slumber. Resting her cheek on the pillow of his broad chest, she breathed his scent and listened to his heart return to a regular rhythm. Heard his breathing settle and knew he'd fallen asleep.

So easy for him, she thought. He probably went to sleep with strange women beside him all the time. Why would it be any different with her?

Because he'd told her he'd never brought a woman here to sleep.

She lifted her head to watch him and her heart tumbled. He looked like the boy she'd known, innocent and sweet. Rather than disturb him, she kissed her fingers, laid them lightly against his lips.

When had she ever felt this fulfilled? The answer was easy. Never. Maybe it was because she'd never made love before in so many ways. Body, mind, heart.

But fear snuck through the hazy contentment. If she wasn't very, very careful her heart would be the loser. Big-time. She wasn't going to let anyone hurt her again. Not Dane, not anyone.

She could not allow uncontrolled emotions and past dreams to cloud what was supposed to be a practical arrangement.

And yet she'd allowed him to set this dangerous precedent by bringing her to his bed tonight. She should have insisted he take her to her own room. She'd leave. In a moment. Carefully sliding off him, she shifted to the edge of the bed, closed her eyes to shut out the reminder of his robe hanging on the back of his door.

Somehow she must have slept, because when she pried open her eyes again the pearly light of dawn was pushing back the darkness. Dane's body was sprawled against her, a heavy palm resting on one breast. Every place their bodies touched was slicked with sweat. Neither had thought to switch on the air-conditioning and a blanket of thick air swamped them.

Too late to slip away to her own bed now.

The vague tingling low in her belly sharpened and spread upward, tightening her nipples into hard peaks. The large-palmed hand covering her breast obviously registered that fact and squeezed gently, then rolled the sensitive nub between his thumb and finger.

'You're awake.' His hand moved lower—a slow, lazy glide that had her arching into his big body.

'Mmm... Uh...' Heat blasted her skin and her breath caught as he reached between her legs and slid a finger over still swollen flesh. Her whole body throbbed, tensed.

'Good morning.' His eyes, smudged with sleep, smiled at her.

He was doing it again, driving her up. Driving her towards the edge. And she had to admit she liked it—especially when he did that thing with his thumb... She was even prepared to let him play there a little longer...

But she had her own ideas...

Twisting, she dragged her body up and over his until she was sitting astride him. She saw him blink, watched his jaw drop as she grasped his sex in both hands and impaled herself. His eyes weren't sleepy now. They were wide and opaque and involved.

'And a good morning to you, too,' she said. Then she slid down on him in one slow, smooth glide. 'Now, pay attention. It's my turn.'

Dane left for the north of the state later that morning. Because she didn't want to appear needy or clingy

Mariel made sure she'd already left for her little office when it was time for him to leave. Of course she gave him a long goodbye kiss.

She spent the next few days in a frenzy of activity, interviewing potential tailors, sketching new designs and preparing patterns.

He called her every night. She missed him. She tried hard not to, because sooner or later he was going to call it off. She knew that. So she focused on her work. The way to success was so clear she could almost taste it.

Unless…

Instead of writing up her order for new stock one morning, she forced herself to confront the impossible and made an appointment with her family doctor. She'd finished the active tablets in her packet of Pills. Her period was nearly two weeks overdue. She didn't want to start a new pack until she knew why.

Dr Judy explained, 'If you haven't missed a Pill, vomited or used other medication, it's unlikely you're pregnant, Mariel.'

Mariel bit down on her lip while she looked at the older woman who'd treated her for all the childhood illnesses over the years, and felt like throwing up. She'd read the Pill's accompanying leaflet. She knew the advice by heart… Now. And *now* was a little late. A lot late. 'I was airsick on the way back to Australia. And somehow I miscalculated the time difference and ended up with a spare Pill…'

Dr Judy scribbled something on Mariel's case notes, then smiled at her over her rimless glasses in a grand-motherly way that made Mariel want to crawl onto her

lap and cry like she'd done when she was five and she'd
had stitches in her knee.

'In that case,' she said, 'why don't we do a blood
test?'

CHAPTER ELEVEN

PREGNANT.

Mariel dived off the edge of Dane's pool and sliced through the blue water with smooth, powerful strokes. Pregnant. She increased her speed as if she could outpace her problem.

Dr Judy had assured her it was a definite positive, and outlined the next steps Mariel should take. Choice of hospital, antenatal classes, vitamins. She'd directed her to a couple of websites that showed images of the foetus virtually from the first week. Imagine that?

Except Mariel could barely remember a thing. A shocked numbness had invaded her body so thoroughly she'd driven back on autopilot and wondered how she'd made it from the hills town of Stirling to the city without an accident. Now, with the refreshing sensation of cool water over her, the shock was dissipating and stark reality was creeping in.

Flipping, she backstroked her way to the middle of the pool, focusing on the sky's cloudless blue bowl above her, keeping her mind on her breathing, her strokes.

Not focusing on the place in the centre of her belly that suddenly seemed to practically pulse with its own

self-awareness. She couldn't think about the baby...
Oh, God, she was having a baby. Dane's baby.

'Dane,' she murmured. The man who didn't want
marriage, who didn't want children.

The man she loved.

Rolling over, she dived deep, listening to the cascade
of bubbles past her ears, trying desperately to outrush
her emotions. She knew how dramatically everything
was going to change.

At the moment Dane was blissfully ignorant, and
likely to remain that way for the next couple of days.
There was no way she could tell him something that important, that devastating, over the phone. She wondered
how long she should let that state of ignorance last.
Maybe she could get away with it a little longer while
she decided the best way to tell him.

But a secret like that wouldn't be a secret for long.

Finally exhausted, she swiped water from her face
as she pushed up out of the water and onto the deck.
She shook her head, scattering water, then wrapped her
hair in a towel and sat on the edge of the pool.

He'd think she'd manipulated him, the way his former
lover had. He'd been prepared to use contraception but
she'd told him she was on the Pill. He couldn't have
made it clearer that he didn't intend having kids. Ever.

So she'd make it clear she didn't intend to force him
into something that would bring unhappiness to both of
them. To all of them. Anger, resentment, and finally in-
difference would follow. And nobody had the right to
bring a child into the world to live under those circumstances. Of all people, Dane would understand that.

A sense of surrealism surrounded her as she reached
for another towel and, wrapping it around her body,

trudged upstairs to take a long, cleansing frangipani-scented bath. She still hadn't examined her own feelings—couldn't. Deliberately she didn't look at her naked body in the mirror as she turned on the taps. Her maternal instinct must have gone AWOL, or maybe it was simply self-preservation or denial, because she could *not* touch her belly and think about the miracle happening in there.

And she had two days to get used to the idea before Dane came home.

In Alice Springs Dane keyed in his home number and switched on his laptop the moment he reached his hotel room. It had become a nightly ritual at seven p.m. over the past week. They'd talk a moment and then, if the reception was clear, switch to computers, where they could see each other while they talked over the day.

It had been a buzz, watching the animation in her face as she told him about her steady journey towards realising her goals. And it gave him an added buzz knowing he'd helped.

Tonight anticipation surged through him. He'd worked it so that he could go home earlier. This time tomorrow he'd be able to say hello to her in the flesh—a surprise he wanted to keep.

He'd never had a woman waiting for him at home. A smile tugged at his lips. Not that Mariel was the kind of woman to wait around.

But tonight she took longer than usual answering. 'Hello?'

Her voice was breathless and intimate and right up close against his ear, but he picked up on something else, too. He couldn't identify it, but it sent a chill skit-

tering over his spine despite the hotel room's ambience.
'Hi, there, Queen Bee.'

'Dane… Oh…is it seven o'clock already?'

'You sound out of breath. Where were you?'

'I was…in the pool.'

He dismissed the hesitation as breathlessness—she'd
told him she was swimming, hadn't she?

'Turn on the computer,' he said. 'I want to see you.'

Definite hesitation this time. 'You want me to leave
a trail of water on the stairs, too?'

'It'll be worth it, I promise.'

'Not tonight,' she said. 'I'm not feeling the best.'

He blew out a slow breath, swallowed his disap-
pointment. 'I'm sorry to hear that. What's wrong?'

'I must have picked up a bug or something.'

'Why don't you take something for it, climb into bed
and get some sleep?'

'I already am. Will be.'

He frowned. Less than a minute ago she'd said she'd
been in the pool. They'd never lied to each other. At
least he hadn't lied to her. They'd promised each other
open and honest communication. What had changed
that? 'Are you sure that's all it is?'

'Yes, I'm sure.'

'I'll say goodnight, then, and let you get some rest.'

'Okay. Goodnight.'

The way she disconnected he could have sworn he
heard the bedside table rattle halfway across Australia.
If she *was* in bed? Something had rattled. He felt a
little rattled himself.

He stretched out on the hotel's crisp quilt cover. Yes,
she was in bed, he assured himself. In *his* bed. Apart
from that last night they'd shared, she'd not slept the

night with him in his home, yet he could see her there as clearly as if he were lying next to her.

Her dark hair, smelling of flowers, fanned out across his pillow and tickling his nose. Moon-glow spilling through the tall window, painting her glorious silk-clad body silver.

But in that same moon-glow he saw a single crystal tear track down her cheek.

His smile faded.

Dane thanked the chauffeur, unfolded his body and stepped out onto the footpath in the late-afternoon sun. Outwardly, his home looked the same as it always did.

Ah, but inside there was a woman, delicate and strong, beautiful and sometimes aloof, that he couldn't wait to see.

Dumping his gear inside the front door, he walked through the house, seeing evidence of Mariel's presence: her handbag, an international designer jacket draped over a chair. She'd cooked something with chilli and cumin and coriander, the aroma reminding him he hadn't enjoyed home cooking in over a week.

In all his adult years he'd never come home to another living soul. He'd learned independence and self-reliance the hard way. He needed no one; he was satisfied with his own company. But this...contentment was all he could think about. Having someone waiting for him, that was something new.

He stopped at the glass door that led to the patio. Mariel was wearing a sexy one-piece crimson swimsuit and lying in the shade on a slatted recliner with a magazine over her face.

His heart constricted. Not painfully, but quietly, with

certainty. As if it knew something he didn't. Which gave him a second's pause. Had her strange mood of last night altered?

Impatient to find out, he stepped onto the sun-drenched patio. A wave of heat rolled up from the decking, enveloping him in the smell of chlorinated water and sun-bleached wood.

He crossed the deck soundlessly, sat on the shaded recliner beside her so that their hips bumped, and slid the magazine from her face. 'Hello, gorgeous.'

Sleepy eyes blinked up at him. He watched emotions flicker through their depths as awareness crystallised. Pleasure, then confusion…and something like dismay. But her voice was composed when she said, 'Either you're a day early or I've been sleeping here a lot longer than I thought.'

He grinned. 'I managed to finish up early.' He laid his hand on her belly.

Her eyes instantly flared at his touch, and if he didn't know Mariel better he would have said he saw a glint of something close to fear in their depths.

'I was concerned about you last night.' Justifiably so, he thought now, as she jerked. Her stomach muscles tightened beneath his palm before she swung her legs onto the deck and stood, facing away from him. He stood, too, to meet her on an equal footing.

'No need,' she said breezily, then turned, smiling, and waggled manicured fingers at him in a flippant manner. Too flippant. 'I'm fine. I just wasn't up for talking.'

This woman standing before him wasn't the Mariel he knew. What had changed her? Something like panic flitted through his system. 'You want to explain why?'

Narrowing his eyes, he scoured her features against the low sun's glare. That perfect but slightly aloof smile was her trademark, the smile she showed the world. It wasn't the one he wanted to see. Not here alone with her. Not as her lover.

He wanted to see the smile that lit a glow in her cheeks and sparked fireworks in her eyes, that emanated a soft radiance that filled up an entire room. The smile that shut the rest of the world out and made him the centre of her universe.

'Not particularly,' she said. 'Not right now.'

Since her voice had grown husky on the last words and she was still smiling, albeit not the smile he wanted to see, he took that as an invitation and moved closer, ready to forgive and forget if he could just reacquaint himself with the taste of her mouth.

He refused to try and interpret the tremble he felt in her lips as they met his. He coaxed her gently, cupping her neck, angling her jaw for a better fit when he felt her spine soften, her body turn pliant. Her hands crept to his shoulders, curving around his neck like ropes of silk.

Satisfaction slid through him on a rising tide of desire. He could lure her with one persuasive kiss. Wasn't she already right here with him? All the way?

He hauled her against his burgeoning erection, her damp bathers slick and cool against the front of his T-shirt, and his hands tingled at the thought of how her skin would feel when he peeled the fabric from her.

She moaned against his mouth, whatever was bothering her obviously forgotten as she poured herself into the kiss, arching against him so that he splayed one hand against her back to support her.

Everything forgotten as he lifted his mouth from her lips to roam across the smooth curves of her face. Cheeks, eyes, brow, jaw. Her long twist of ebony hair slithered damply over his forearm; her fingers dug little grooves into his neck.

Now, *this* was coming home. While he could still stand, he leaned down and, with one arm beneath her knees, swept her into his arms and headed for the door.

Her softly fluttering eyes were startled open.

'Relax,' he said, kissing her brow as he reached the staircase. 'I've decided that from now on carrying you upstairs is going to become part of my daily exercise routine.'

Mariel's heart stuttered. Not when he knew what she had to tell him, it wouldn't.

Steel eyes met hers as his footsteps stalled on the stairs. 'What's wrong?'

'I smell like chlorine,' she whispered. 'My hair's still wet.'

'You think I care?'

'I guess not...' Weak with wanting, and powerless to resist what she knew was coming, she allowed herself to be carried up the stairs—again—like some modern-day Scarlett O'Hara.

Because she knew it would be the last time.

One last time to know how it felt to be made love to by Dane.

The sheen of the day's heat reflected on the ivory-coloured walls as he laid her on his bed.

Yanking his T-shirt over his head, he stripped naked in ten seconds flat, then crawled onto the bed. She'd never seen such passion in his eyes as he slid the straps of her bathers over her shoulders and down her arms.

Her nipples, already hard from desire and damp, puckered further as he drew the fabric away.

Then he was tugging it from beneath her bottom and sliding it down over her thighs, her knees, her ankles. He reached out, traced the curve of one breast. 'I'd say you were beautiful, but you've heard it before.'

Mariel heard the casual tone, rather than the compliment, and her heart constricted. 'Not from you, I haven't. Not this way.'

His eyes met hers, a long, lingering hold that imprisoned her with silent and steely intensity.

'So tell me.' Her voice was edgy with impatience. Just once, she wanted to hear it from Dane's lips.

His eyes crinkled up around the edges for a moment, then his expression turned serious once more. 'Ninety-nine percent of the time beauty's an accident of birth. That's what men see when they look at you. So when I tell you you're beautiful I'm not only talking about the softness of your skin or the colour of your eyes. It's inside you, Queen Bee, where it counts.'

As he spoke, his palm seared her skin, rubbing slowly beneath her left breast, then over her concave belly.

Over his unborn child.

Tears gathered in her heart. She wanted to weep. She sensed something more in Dane's voice today. More in his eyes, more in his kiss. Over the past few days her vision had cleared, as if a curtain had been lifted. It didn't matter that they argued and disagreed. That there'd always be vocal and noisy differences of opinion. Who was right and who was in control?

It didn't matter.

Under different circumstances she'd have asked him if it was the same for him, no hesitation. If nothing else they'd always had trust and honesty between them. With time and patience *maybe* she could have had it all, but she'd carelessly thrown that chance away. Because there was no negotiation where children and Dane were concerned.

So take this moment and this man, she told herself. Take the rest of tonight and make it special. Memorable.

She might possibly die of a broken heart, but his was made of stone and she'd told him so and he hadn't denied it. He'd be okay. He'd get over the shock and the anger and they'd sort everything out, and maybe they could still be friends the way they'd always been.

Friends sharing a child. That wasn't so impossible. Was it?

'Perhaps I shouldn't have told you after all,' he murmured in his deep, husky voice, and she realised her mind had wandered off. 'It seems to have made you sad.'

She shook her head against the pillow. 'Make love with me,' she whispered. 'No one ever made love with me the way you do.'

He bent his head, grazed her lips once, twice. 'Because no one knows you the way I do.'

She wanted to tell him she loved him, right here, right now, while the moment sparkled with truth. But the only truth around here tonight was his truth. And her untold secret proved him wrong. He didn't know her as well as he thought. It spun a web of guilt around her, but when he covered her body with his she lifted her arms and gave herself up to him.

Tonight was lingering looks, slow, sweet passion, the languid glide of flesh on flesh. A lazy touch. A tender kiss. She took him inside her wordlessly and with all the love she had to give.

The lowering sun turned the room orange, his skin to bronze. His eyes were dark, almost black in the fading light, and his day's worth of stubble shadowed his jaw and rasped against her hand when she reached out to absorb, to stroke.

Dane became her only reality in a room she no longer saw. The sound of his murmurs, the thump of his heart against hers. The intoxicating scent of man. This man.

And she clung to that reality, to Dane, and in those all too short precious moments, lived that lifetime she was going to be denied.

CHAPTER TWELVE

MARIEL woke first. It was full dark, and the city's twinkling lights cast a dim glow across the walls. Angry with herself for falling asleep, she turned to watch Dane. She'd wanted to stay awake and think. To lie beside him and listen to his breathing while she prepared herself to tell him.

As if he sensed she was awake, his eyes blinked open in the semi-darkness. 'Hi.'

'Hi.'

He moved an arm, stopped. Then pulled a silk night-gown from beneath him and dangled it in front of her with a grin. 'What's this?'

'Oh...' Mariel felt herself flush. 'I...'

Damn it, she hadn't expected him back tonight, and now her secret indulgence to sleep where he slept and feel close to him was out in the open for Dane's scrutiny.

'You slept in my bed.' It wasn't a question.

'Yes. Is that a hanging offence?'

He kissed the tip of her nose. 'I don't think so. Wait here.' He slid off the bed and disappeared downstairs.

He was back in less than a minute with a small swing bag. He switched on the bedside lamp, filling the room with a soft ambience. 'A present from Alice Springs.' The mattress dipped as he climbed back onto the bed with her.

With trembling fingers she pulled out a sexy black bra and matching thong. Her heart soared briefly, then sank as she stroked the flimsy material. How long would she be able to wear it? 'Thank you, they're beautiful. How did you know what size?'

His eyes twinkled and he cupped a breast in his palm. 'You think I don't know the size of your breasts by now?'

'I guess you do. They're lovely.' He didn't suggest she model them, thank heavens, and she set them aside. The tremor in her fingers increased. 'Dane…'

'Mmm?' He shifted closer, nibbled her shoulder. 'I'm hungry; how about you?'

She breathed a tremulous sigh of partial relief. Off the hook a little longer. And they needed to eat before she knuckled down and told him. 'I could do with a cheeseburger and fries.'

His brows rose. 'You want junk food? You never eat junk food.'

'I do. Just not often.'

'What was that yummy dish I smelled in the kitchen when I came home?'

'I didn't know you were coming; there's only enough for one.'

'We could share…'

'We could. But you'd still be hungry. And I haven't cooked the rice yet. It'll take—'

'Okay, okay, I get the message. Pull on some clothes and we'll do take-away.'

* * *

Dane wanted to take their meal and sit by the River Torrens, where it was cooler, and watch the lights reflect on the water. But Mariel didn't seem keen, so they ate at home on the sofa in front of the TV. She was giving her earlobe a workout and his unease flooded back.

When he'd finished his meal, and eaten Mariel's half-finished burger, he stuffed the cardboard containers back into the carry-bag, tossed it on the table. He shifted to a forty-five-degree angle so that he could see her properly. 'Okay, Mariel, what's the problem?'

She bit on her lip, then lifted her chin, took a breath. 'You're not going to like this…'

His stomach bottomed out, but he remained outwardly calm. 'Try me.'

She heaved another breath, as if garnering courage. 'I'm pregnant.'

His brain took a couple of seconds to process the information. It took another couple to get his tongue to work around the word he'd never imagined associated with their lives. His life. 'Pregnant.'

His vision blurred, and the only sound he could hear was the rasp of air as it caught on his tonsils on its way to his rapidly deflating lungs. 'Pregnant.' He blinked to clear the haze that he found himself enshrouded in and saw Mariel, pale-faced, eyes too big, too vulnerable, her hands clenched tightly in her lap.

'Yes.' She worried her bottom lip again. 'I found out yesterday.'

Rational thought began to surface, along with denial. 'How is that possible? I thought you were on the Pill? That's what you told me.' He heard the accusation in his own voice.

Déjà vu. Flashback to another woman, another time. Had Mariel planned it? He shook it away immediately.

'I *was* on the Pill…' She rubbed her arms as if cold. 'I was due to start another packet but I never got my period. So I went to see Dr Judy at Stirling to ask her advice.'

Unable to sit, he pushed up and paced. 'So when you told me last night that you had a bug, you were lying?'

'I couldn't tell you that kind of news over the phone. You would *not* have wanted me to tell you over the phone. Something this important has to be said face to face.'

He acknowledged that with a stiff-necked nod. 'So, what are your plans?'

'*My* plans?' Her eyes narrowed. 'Oh, that's just great. So it seems when things get too hard you're a typical irresponsible male after all. This is your baby, too, so it's *our* plans. Like it or not, this is about *us.*'

'You're missing my intention. I'm giving *you* the option. It's your call. But you'll have my full support whatever you decide.'

She stared at him. 'You…you…' She pushed off the sofa, all white-faced fury, and stood before him, fingers clenching and unclenching at her sides. 'If you're thinking what I think you're thinking—'

'You haven't a clue what I'm thinking,' he shot back. 'How could you when I don't know what the hell I'm thinking myself?' Why did she have to look at him that way, her eyes brimming with tears and censure? 'Oh, no… No, Mariel, I didn't mean…'

And then it hit him—a bolt from the sky, a tsunami, a super cyclone all rolled into one.

His baby.

A part of him.

Growing inside Mariel.

Adrenaline spiked through his veins and bled like fire into already tight muscles. His heart pumped so hard he thought he'd burst a valve.

Seemingly of their own volition his eyes sought and found Mariel's flat belly. Hidden beneath a lolly-pink mini-skirt…his baby.

Some insane, primitive part of him wanted to beat his chest and shout it to the ends of the earth. He dragged his eyes away and turned to stare blindly at the night-darkened window, his mind assaulted by a barrage of *what-the-hell-do-I-do-now?* scenarios.

He could feel her eyes drilling into his back. She was waiting for more from him, expecting more from him. And she *should* expect more. 'I have to think.' Shoving his hands through his hair, he locked them behind his head as he continued to stare into the night. 'I need to get my head around this.'

He heard the shift of fabric and a soft footfall on the polished boards. Something like panic gripped him at the thought that she'd leave without a word and, worse, that he'd allow it.

'Mariel…' He crossed to her in four quick strides, grabbed her fingers. Her hands felt chilled, the bones fragile. He ran his thumb over them and looked into her over-bright eyes. 'When I suggested this arrangement I thought it would help you.'

Mariel saw his pain etched in every furrow, every facial muscle, felt it echo in her heart. She knew he was in shock. That he was still a long way from dealing with the news. But he hadn't told her what she wanted to hear. *We'll get married.* Or even, *I won't leave you* or *We'll raise it together.* And why would he? They'd never agreed to that. And now he'd be leaving not one person but two people.

Pressing her lips together, she nodded, unable to speak lest she blubber—and she didn't want to blubber and reveal how desperately needy she felt right now. How much she wanted him to hold her closer and kiss her and tell her everything was going to be all right.

But it wasn't going to be all right. Because no matter how close they were, or how much she loved him, when it came to the important ever-after stuff they were at opposite ends of the spectrum.

He squeezed her hands once, passed a whispered caress across her lips. 'Go on to bed. You need to take care of yourself now. I'll see you in the morning.'

His kiss was as sweet as ever, and he sounded as sincere as he always did, but a chasm had opened up between them and she knew they'd ever be the same again.

The following morning Dane left before Mariel was awake. He might have opened the door to check on her, but she didn't hear him. She tried to focus on work. She'd need some sort of income to maintain her independence. She didn't have a clue about where she'd live, what Dane would provide—if anything—so she couldn't make plans.

You'll have my full support. His words. But how far did that extend? she wondered. And what had he meant? Financial? Emotional?

Bringing her pregnancy out in the open with him seemed to have sparked her maternal instinct. She thought of Dane's mother, who'd left him. Did the woman not realise all she'd missed out on?

Well, Mariel didn't intend to miss out on a minute of

raising her baby. She'd always dreamed of kids of her own, a man who loved her to share the joy with. But if the father wasn't going to be around, so be it. She'd still have a little reminder of Dane that she could love for ever.

Everything was on hold, like suspended animation. She hated it, but she marked time. She had to wait. Maybe tonight. Would he come and tell her he'd decided he wanted to make a go of it?

But when he came home from the office it was eight o'clock, and she was already in bed, emotionally and physically exhausted. She heard his footsteps hesitate outside her door, then he moved on.

No. She wouldn't let herself weep for the man she loved and would walk away from. Nor was she going to wait around for him to make a decision. She had some pride left, and she refused to be a victim again.

Slipping out of bed, she opened her door. Light from his study cast a strip of light across the polished boards in the passage. Placing one foot in front of the other, she moved towards it.

His phone rang as she was about to enter.

'Huntington.' Pause. 'Yes. I meant to get back to you. There's—' He rolled his head back and studied the ceiling. 'Tonight?' From behind him Mariel saw him rub his temple. 'Okay.' He glanced at his watch. 'Twenty minutes. Don't worry, I'll be there.'

A faint creak in the floorboards alerted him to Mariel's presence. His hand jerked—almost guiltily, she thought—then he disconnected and slipped the phone in his pocket. 'I thought you were asleep, I didn't want to wake you.'

'You didn't wake me. I wanted to talk.'

'I would, but I'm sorry, now's not a good time. I've got an urgent matter I need to deal with.'

She felt her mouth go dry, felt her tongue stick to the roof of her mouth, but she managed to say, 'Now? What's more important than our baby?'

Dane stilled, and something flickered behind the still gaze. 'We'll talk. We will. But it's business. A client.'

'A client.'

'Don't do this, Mariel.' He turned away to shut down his computer, then riffled through an untidy pile of papers. 'You'll have to trust me on this.'

Trust him? The way she'd trusted Luc? He'd had 'business appointments', too. She fought back tears.

He rose and, still folding whatever it was he'd been looking for, walked towards her. He tilted her chin up, gripped it between tense fingers. '*Do* you trust me?'

She thought of his women, his playboy lifestyle. She remembered their childhood and shared secrets, the last couple of weeks they'd spent together here in his home. Arguing, making love. She wanted to trust him. How she wanted to. He was her baby's father; nothing could change that fact. And they were bound by it for the rest of their lives.

'Well?' he demanded. His eyes swirled with some emotion she couldn't read.

'If we don't have trust, Dane, we have nothing.' She couldn't deny it. She couldn't deny him the chance to prove it. If she didn't, there was no future for them at all.

His shoulders relaxed as some of the tension there eased. 'Go to bed. Get some sleep. You look like you need it.' The kiss he laid on her lips was sweet but brief.

Whether he crept in without a sound or whether she was sleeping—though she was sure she'd not slept a wink—Mariel didn't hear him come home.

CHAPTER THIRTEEN

THE following day started out as the day from hell and grew worse with every passing hour. Mariel heard the wind pick up soon after dawn, seething through the casuarinas over the road. From her bedroom window she could see that the sky had turned a dull brown, with raised dust obscuring the rising sun.

Dane left soon after. She waited until she heard his car start, then went downstairs. She tried to eat, but even the thought of putting anything in her stomach made her feel ill. The onset of morning sickness? she wondered.

The radio's weather bulletin was dire. Forty-five degrees, with gale force winds. Hills residents were being advised to ensure their bushfire action plans were in place: to leave now, or stay and be prepared to fight if a fire broke out. It was shaping up to be a day reminiscent of Black Saturday, that horrific day Victoria had burned.

Mid-morning the phone rang. 'Ah, Mariel,' the agitated voice said when she picked up. 'Daniel Huntington here. Is Dane about?'

'He's not here, Daniel. Have you tried his office or his mobile?'

'He's not answering either of those numbers.'

The tone of his voice worried Mariel as she rubbed absently at her empty tummy. 'Are you all right? Is there something I can help you with?'

'It's blowing like the devil up here. I don't like the looks of it, Mariel. Bloody arsonists about. One spark…'

She closed her eyes and wished she didn't have to offer, but… 'Why don't you come down here for the day?'

His blunt, 'I'm not leaving the house,' worried her more.

'It's only a house, Daniel. Material things can be replaced. You're what matters.'

'This is Dane's house, and I'm not leaving it to burn down.'

Dane's house? What did he mean by that? 'There's no fire there now, is there?' Holding the phone in one hand, she clicked on the Internet to see if there were any reports.

'No. But I was just outside, and damned if I can't smell smoke.' There was a shuffling sound on the line, then a thud.

Mariel pressed the phone closer. 'Are you there, Daniel?'

'I'm here. Just trying to shut…the door. It's blowing like the devil. In these conditions if a fire catches hold, we're done for.'

Mariel chewed on her lip in an agony of indecision. He was in his seventies and alone, and in the danger zone on a major bushfire alert day. He sounded out of breath and out of sorts. She couldn't leave him there. She could *not*.

'Listen, Daniel. I'm going to drive up there now and pick you up.'

'No, girlie, I'm not leaving.'

'Okay,' she said, keeping her voice low and soothing. 'I'll come, and we'll talk when I get there.'

Another silence, then a sigh that sounded like relief. 'You're a good woman, Mariel. I'll put the kettle on.'

Mariel disconnected. Great. A joyride to the hills to spend the day from hell with an old man who was as stubborn as his son!

And that old man was her baby's grandfather.

If that wasn't a good enough reason, she didn't know what was.

She tried Dane's phones before she left, to let him know her plans, but the office was still unattended and his mobile was switched off. She knew he had an early breakfast meeting. No point in bothering him now. She'd call him again when she got there and let him know what was going on.

Fifteen minutes later she was on the road.

With a sharp expletive, Dane slammed his foot on the brake. Two elderly women skirted the bonnet, glaring at him as they crossed the driveway outside his office. 'Sorry, ladies.' He smiled an apology. At least he thought his lips moved. They felt a little numb. The oldies kept right on glaring.

'If you'd had as little shut-eye as I have over the past couple of nights you'd be sleep-walking, too,' he muttered.

He waited till they'd taken their sweet time, then zoomed into his personal parking space, killed the engine and let his head roll back on the headrest. His seven-thirty a.m. meeting with a new client had finished early, which now gave him time to check in at the office before heading out again for another meeting and to upgrade a system east of the city.

Not far from the freeway, he thought. His conscience pricked at him. Inconvenient thing, conscience. But he'd drive out to see his father afterwards, just to check he was okay on this hellish day. Wouldn't take long.

Justin's car was nowhere to be seen, and their shared PA was on leave for another week, so the office blinds were shut against the heat, the rooms relatively cool and dim when he entered. He sank into the plush chair behind his desk, checked the office phone and mobile for messages. He returned three calls, left a message in answer to another.

That done, he stuck his feet on his desk and closed his eyes. But he couldn't find the relief he sought. *Mariel.* Her name rippled across his mind like cool, clean water. He should have made time for her, but somehow he just hadn't been able to deal with it. Pain crawled up his chest and into his throat. Worse, he'd let her down when she most needed him.

'Jeez, man, you look like crap.'

His eyes jerked open at the familiar voice. Justin, wearing a fresh white business shirt and pressed trousers, frowned at him from the doorway. He screwed them shut again. 'Go away, Jus.'

'No can do. I'm your business partner, mate.'

Dane could feel his disapproval clear across the room. When he didn't leave, Dane opened his eyes. 'What?'

'Don't tell me you just tried to woo a new client in that sorry excuse for a T-shirt.'

'Okay, I won't tell you.'

'What's with the excess facial fuzz? And the hair— isn't it about time for a trim? A little professional—'

'If I need someone to nag me I'll get a wife,' he

snarled. He picked up a rubber band, stretched it till it broke and snapped against his fingers. He welcomed its sting.

Justin walked right into the room, rested one hip on the corner of Dane's desk. 'Does Mariel realise what she's let herself in for?'

'If she doesn't like the arrangement she's free to leave. In fact I'm expecting the kiss-off any time now. I'll be sure to let you know when it happens, so you won't worry about her.' He snatched up another rubber band, aimed it at the trophy on top of his filing cabinet and fired. 'Probably be the best decision she ever made.'

'Blimey, Dane.'

Dane glanced at his friend, then had to turn away from the accusation he read in his eyes. 'You know me. Commitment was never my strong suit.'

'A blind fool can see that you love her. She only has to walk into the room and that steel in your eyes melts. What the hell happened?'

A baby happened.

Nerves jittered. His heart tightened. 'Fact is, I…' he began, but his vocal cords wouldn't work properly. 'Fact is, we…' He swallowed over the lump in his throat.

Suddenly everything fell into place. This baby was an innocent in all this. Dane knew how it was to grow up without a father's love, without any parental affection. He'd learned from it, was stronger because of it. But did he want the same for his own child? Hell, no. He'd been given a chance. A real chance. And he'd been given it with Mariel. His best friend.

The woman he loved more than anything or anyone. Was he just going to let the only genuine woman who had ever entered his life, the only woman who could blow away the storm clouds he saw in his eyes every time he looked in a mirror, walk away? Could he let the child they'd created together grow up without knowing its father? Without a father's love?

Not if he could help it. He'd just been handed the greatest challenge of his life and he wasn't backing down.

He jack-knifed out of his chair, snapping open his mobile while he walked to the door, barely aware of Justin staring at him as if he'd just lost his mind. Maybe he had lost it for a moment, but now he had it back.

'Mate. Friend. You're just what I needed.' With a headflick, he motioned Jus out. 'Excuse me, I need to make a very important call.' Maybe the most important call of his life.

The instant Justin stepped out, Dane slammed the door shut behind him while he punched in his home number. No answer. He slapped a thigh as impatience simmered through him. Now he knew what he had to do he couldn't wait to get on with it. He tried Mariel's mobile. No answer; his call was directed to her voicemail.

Clenching his fist, he paced to the desk and spoke into the phone. 'Mariel, I've been a bloody idiot. Call me when you get this. I need to see you. ASAP.' Something this important had to be said face to face. He checked his watch. Damn. 'On second thought, don't, I've got a meeting coming up. I'll phone you when it's finished.' He closed his eyes. *I love you, Queen Bee.*

Mariel clenched her hands around the steering wheel, struggling to keep the car in a straight line. The thermometer indicated that it was forty-two degrees outside. Even the air-conditioner failed to cool the interior as hot wind snuck in through the cracks and a hazy sun glared through the windscreen. A branch skidded across the road in front of her. Her mouth was dry, but she dared not let her tensed fingers stray from the wheel to reach for her bottled water.

Finally she parked outside Daniel's house. And stepped out into hell on earth.

A relentless January sun had baked the sky bone-white and sucked the earth dry. She stood a few seconds, her pulse stepping up as she stared in rising horror at the shimmering dust haze shrouding the usually beautiful landscape.

A tinderbox. *One spark...*

'Oh, my God,' she murmured. But the wind, a terrifying banshee of blistering heat, whipped the words from her mouth with the same fury as it ripped through trees and sent debris flying through the air like missiles.

She reached the front door, but no one answered her frantic knocks so she ran to the back. Dane's father was lying in the full sun with the hose in his hand, water spraying on the muddy earth beside him. 'Daniel!' she heard herself scream, and dropped to her knees beside him. 'What are you doing out here?'

'Don't want the house to burn. Mariel?' He peered up at her with pale watery eyes.

'There's no fire, Daniel,' she soothed, but her pulse was hammering in her throat. 'Come on.' She tried to tug him up, but he wasn't going anywhere on his own. She levered herself beneath one shoulder and dragged him a few metres into the shade. The effort left her dazed and breathless, but she unscrewed the top on her water and held the bottle to his lips. 'Here, drink.'

He gulped a couple of mouthfuls, then lay back. She poured the rest of the water onto a wad of tissues she found in her bag and wiped his face, then felt for his pulse. It galloped beneath her fingers. She pulled her mobile from her bag and rang for an ambulance. Then she phoned Dane. Damn him, why wasn't his bloody phone on? She left a message to inform him about his father, then hauled herself up, swaying a little as spots danced before her eyes.

'I'll be back in a moment,' she told Daniel, dry-mouthed, then ran inside and found a towel, soaked it in water and rushed back outside.

'You're a good woman for Dane,' he mumbled while she laid the towel across his body. 'Dane's all I have. Should've been a better…father…' He frowned. 'Head hurts.'

'It's going to be okay,' she told him, closing her eyes. But she didn't feel a hundred percent herself, and that queasy feeling was back. 'Help's coming.'

Finally she heard the wail of the siren over the screaming wind. Dragging herself up, she staggered to the driveway to usher the ambulance around the back.

The paramedics jumped out and checked Daniel over. 'Mild heat exhaustion,' the older man said. 'Lucky we got here when we did. Is he your granddad?'

'No. My…partner's father.'

'So you don't live here?'

She shook her head. 'He lives alone. I came by to check on him.'

'Lucky break. We'll take him in for observation, get some fluids into him, but it looks like he's going to be okay.'

The younger guy glanced at her. A small frown

creased his brow, concern in his light blue eyes. 'You okay? Here. Drink this.' He handed her a bottle of water.

'Thanks.' She drank deeply, swiped the sweat off her neck, her face, took a deep steadying breath. She shifted her stance to relieve the dull ache in her abdomen. 'I'll be okay in a minute.' She watched, sliding sweaty palms together while they loaded Daniel into the nearby ambulance.

Dane, where are you?

'Hey,' said a deep voice near her ear. 'I think you should ride along with us and let me check you over, too.'

'I'm fine.' It was like trying to breathe in an oven. Spots danced in front of her eyes. Firm hands helped her up. He passed her handbag to her. 'You want to call your partner? Let him know what's going on?'

She nodded. 'I'll leave a message.'

An hour later she stood looking out at the dust-ravaged panorama from the fourth-floor hospital window while Daniel slept. He was staying in overnight and going to be okay, but he couldn't go back home. He needed rest and care and monitoring over the next few days. And she was going to ask Dane if his father could go home with him. No, she wasn't going to ask. She was going to demand. There were plenty of spare rooms. If necessary he could have her room.

And if Dane refused she'd go home with Daniel herself, if only to show Dane what an idiot he was. What both men were, when it came to that. It was so important for them to re-establish some kind of a relationship. He was going to be her child's grandfather, and somehow it had fallen on her shoulders to take the first steps towards making a family unit, even if that 'unit' was likely to be spread in three different locations across the city.

Abruptly she felt the floor heave beneath her. She sank onto the visitor's chair, blinking away an encroaching grey mist. The twinge she'd barely noticed this morning suddenly took on a more sinister meaning. *No!* Tears gathered in her eyes as the mist grew darker. She'd had little sleep and a rough morning; that was all. That. Was. All.

She reached out and pressed the nurses' call button before she crumpled over.

CHAPTER FOURTEEN

DANE marched through the hospital foyer, his sneakers squeaking on the linoleum, the smell of antiseptic filling his nostrils. He could barely contain his frustration. Mariel hadn't called back—a situation that didn't bode well for the resolution he'd hoped for.

He'd put his heart on the line in that phone call. But obviously that wasn't enough. She expected him to grovel. And right now he was desperate enough to do just that. Once in a lifetime monumental measures were needed to achieve a monumental outcome. He hoped. By God, he hoped.

So while he waited for the elevator he arranged for a delivery of flowers. He made a reservation at one of Mariel's favourite restaurants while the lift carried him to the fourth floor.

At the nurses' station the petite nurse blushed when he smiled at her. He enquired about his father's room, then promptly forgot her. He could be out of here in ten minutes once he saw his father and assured himself the old goat was okay. The problem of care could be sorted out tomorrow—

'You're Mr Daniel Huntington's son?' a voice asked

behind him, before he'd taken more than a few steps. Barely curbing his impatience, Dane turned his head, continued walking. 'Yes.'

'Dane?' It was the same blushing nurse, with her efficient-looking clipboard in her hand, but this time she appeared more flustered than dazzled. 'And Ms Mariel Davenport is your partner?'

His mouth tightened infinitesimally. Had he met her somewhere? A function? He couldn't recall. 'Yes to both questions,' he clipped.

She nodded, Ms Cool and Professional now. 'Will you come with me, please?'

'Is Mariel here?' He stopped, swivelled to look at her.

She didn't meet his eyes; they were focused on the board in her hands. 'If you'll just come with me…'

'Where are we going?' he asked as he entered the elevator with her.

'To the first floor.' She watched the numbers light up as they descended. He sensed her relief when the doors whooshed open. 'Just speak to one the nurses here; they're expecting you,' she said, pointing to the nurses' station. 'They'll answer all your questions.' He stepped out and she shuffled back. He had a fleeting glimpse of her watching him as the doors closed again.

'Hey…' He turned his attention in the direction she'd indicated, saw a couple of staff glance his way, then lean confidentially towards one another, speaking quietly.

He ran a hand around the back of his neck to soothe the sudden tension there then strode towards them. He wanted answers, but he had a gut feeling he wasn't going to like what he heard.

A middle-aged nurse with sheep's wool hair and

purple-rimmed glasses met him halfway. 'Mr Huntington.'

He nodded curtly. 'What's going on?'

'Ms Davenport has been admitted.' She started walking. 'She's through here.'

'Admitted? Why?' he demanded. 'What happened? How is she?' Good God, didn't anyone around here know how to give a straight answer?

'She'll be fine,' the nurse reassured him when he ran out of words, stopping at the door to a private room. 'She's awake. I'll let her tell you.'

He came to a halt beside the bed. Mariel was one strong woman, and seeing her in a pink and white striped hospital gown, hooked up to a drip, face pale, eyes dull, looking vulnerable and lost, nearly brought him to his knees.

He dropped into the visitor's chair. It scraped across the linoleum as he pulled it close. 'What happened—and why the *hell* didn't someone call me?'

'Because I told them not to.' She looked away, to the dull sky thickening with ominous clouds. 'I didn't want to see you. I wanted to be alone. I still want to be alone.'

His chest tightened further. 'No. I'm not letting you be alone, because you don't really mean that.'

'I do.' Her fingers tightened on the sheet. 'You'll be relieved to know I lost the baby.'

No. Not that. A black hole opened inside him. His heart dropped to his shoes. He'd been offered something precious and he'd been too blind to see it until it was too late. Worse, much worse, he'd hurt the woman he loved with his unspeakably selfish behaviour. 'Mariel. Sweetheart…I'm sorry.' Such inadequate words to express the mountain of emotion, his pain.

Her pain.

He took her hand, chafed it between his. It felt small and fragile, the way she looked right now. She never looked fragile. But at this moment she did. Her face was too pale, her eyes too haunted. 'If I could change anything in the world I'd turn back time—just one day, if that's all I could have, and start over.'

She lifted a shoulder. 'A pretty fairytale. So why say it? Because you think you might magically change your mind about being a father? Hardly. Because you think it'll make me feel better? It doesn't.'

He leaned closer, breathed in the scent of her skin. 'When I rang you it was because I wanted to see you. I wanted to tell you something important.'

'You didn't ring me.'

'I left a voice message. You didn't get it?'

She shook her head and her lips thinned. 'It may have escaped your attention, but I was far too busy dealing with an emergency to check for messages. Your father could have died out there alone today.'

'He didn't—thanks to you.'

'So…what was it that was so *important*?' She weighted the last word and turned away as she spoke. Her cold dismissal was like a kick in the gut.

'Damn it, Mariel.' He pulled her bag from the bedside locker, switched on her phone. 'Here.' He shoved it in her hand. 'Listen.'

He watched her face. Nothing but cool remoteness in her eyes. 'So…the "bloody idiot" bit I already know. Apart from that, your message doesn't tell me a thing.'

'You didn't pay attention to the way it was delivered. What I really wanted to say couldn't be said over the phone. And you understand that as well as I.'

She gave an infinitesimal nod. 'Okay. Tell me now.'

'I wanted to tell you that I wanted to make a life with you and the bab—' He bit his tongue so hard he tasted blood.

He saw her chest—a quick movement, as if she'd gasped—but her face remained an impassive mask, her eyes fixed somewhere outside the window.

Appalled. He was appalled. 'I'm sorry. But I meant what I said. With all my heart, I meant what I said.'

A long silence filled the room. 'It's easy to say that *now*, isn't it?'

'You think it's *easy*?' He jerked off the chair, pushed his hands through his hair and told the ceiling, 'Nothing with you is easy.'

Frustration consumed him. He could understand where she was coming from. With no pregnancy, his words were empty words. No longer applicable. Some might say he was off the hook.

He didn't want to be cast off. He wanted everything back the way it had been this morning. With the woman he intended spending the rest of his life with, raising their child.

And somehow he was going to make at least the first part happen.

He spun back to the bed, sat down on the covers and reached for her hand. A sense of urgency hammered at him. He had a plan, a last chance, but he needed a little time to put it into action. 'You saved Dad, sweetheart. Life is priceless.'

'Yes. It is.' Her eyes filled. 'Do something for me.'

'Anything.'

'Go and see your father.'

He nodded, pressed a kiss to her cheek. 'I'll be back.'

* * *

'Dad.' Dane sat down beside the old man. 'You've had an eventful day, I hear.'

His father opened his eyes. 'Dane.' His bony shoulders visibly relaxed and his papery lips curved just a little.

'And we have Mariel to thank for that.' He clenched his jaw around the words.

'She's a jewel of a girl, that one.'

So...his dad didn't know Mariel had collapsed in his room? 'She is. So what the hell were you doing, watering the garden in forty-plus degrees?'

'Protecting *your* assets. One spark and it could've all been gone.'

'I never asked you to protect it,' Dane growled, then softened when he saw his father's expression. 'It's just a house, Dad. I've been thinking of selling it. Too many bad memories.'

His father's eyes searched his, then he nodded, seemingly defeated.

Dane picked up the water pitcher, refilled his father's glass. 'You shouldn't be there on your own. You could move down to the city. North Adelaide. Lots of history. Convenient. Plenty of parks and shopping close by.'

'Well, now.' He scratched his jaw. 'Maybe.'

Dane wandered to the window and looked out over the night-drenched Botanic Gardens, crouched in shadow. Heard himself saying, 'Plenty of spare rooms at my place.'

A long silence. 'You'd do that? For me? After everything that's happened?'

The wonder, the hope in his father's voice, made him

want to reach out. He dug his hands in the back pockets of his jeans. 'Maybe.'

His father had made the first move on the night of the ball. They'd made progress over that game of chess. 'It would come with conditions.' He turned to his father, but didn't step closer. 'The brewer who had the house built back in the 1870s raised nine children there. It's a good old-fashioned family home. With good old-fashioned family values.' He nodded to his father and walked to the door. 'Think long and hard about that.'

'Good morning, Mariel.' A young nurse with a mass of red hair and a row of studs in her left ear set a tray on the bedside table. 'My name's Tara and I'll be looking after you this morning.'

'Good morning.' Pushing her hair out of her eyes, Mariel glanced at the clock. 'Six o'clock already? That sedative last night put me right out.'

'The doctor didn't prescribe you a sedative last night.' Tara smiled as she did her morning obs and jotted notes on the clipboard at the foot of the bed. 'Spare a thought for your poor guy. He didn't look like he'd slept a wink.'

Mariel knew that look. Long mussed hair, thirteen-o'clock shadow. Soft mouth, hang-dog eyes that made you want to push him back onto the mattress, cuddle into that warmth and make love till—

'Dane was here?'

Tara lowered the sheet. 'All night on that chair, according to the night nurse. You just missed him. He left about twenty minutes ago.'

He must have gone home at some point, Mariel realised, because she spotted her cosmetic bag and a change of clothes on the shelf in front of the mirror.

Tara pulled the sheet back up, patted Mariel's leg. 'Bleeding's stopped.'

'Does that mean I can go home today?' she asked, with a listless glance towards the window. Where was home? She no longer knew.

'Dr Martinez will let you know when she makes her rounds this morning. She's requested a blood test first,' she said, preparing a syringe.

Mariel leaned back against the pillow. 'Oh, goody.'

'And then she wants you to have an ultrasound.'

A short time later Mariel watched the unreadable image on the monitor.

'Baby?' Mariel stared at the monitor, then looked at the technician. 'I'm still pregnant?'

'You are. It's not recognisable yet,' the technician said. 'But see this thickening here?'

'I'm still pregnant?' Her heart thundered with renewed hope. With joy. 'But I had bleeding…' She couldn't read the blur, but she couldn't take her eyes off the monitor.

Dane. What would he say now? What would *she* say?

Dr Martinez appeared at her side. 'Good morning.' She turned to look at Mariel. 'How are you feeling this morning?'

'Last night I was told I'd had a miscarriage.' To her shame, tears welled up and rolled down her cheeks, and her voice trembled when she said, 'Will someone please explain what's going on?'

'You were carrying twins,' Dr Martinez explained. 'One foetus aborted, but the other one's fine.'

Mariel rubbed her chest to ease the nerves rioting

through her system. 'I've never heard of anyone having a miscarriage and still being pregnant. Is that normal? Is it dangerous?'

'It happens. It's known as Vanishing Twin Syndrome,' Dr Martinez explained. 'With IVF now, and very early monitoring, we're finding it happens more often than we once thought.'

Still unconvinced, Mariel looked back at the monitor. 'Is this one at risk now?'

The doctor touched Mariel's hand. 'There's no reason why it shouldn't be a normal pregnancy. And the other good news is you can go home this morning.'

At nine-thirty the nurse entered Mariel's room to bring in the discharge forms for her to sign. She was ready to go home, but where would 'home' be for her now? 'Thanks, Tara.'

Tara smiled and placed the papers on the table. Mariel stood at the window, looking out at the misty rain. Some time last night the cool change had blown in. She ran a damp palm down the side of the dress Dane had brought in with its matching jacket and paced back to the bed. She was jittery. Tara had told her Dane had left strict instructions at the nurses' station that she was not to leave until he came to fetch her.

She had to tell him about the baby.

She had to go through that agonising moment again.

'Are you and your fiancé planning on having kids?' she asked Tara as the nurse walked to the door.

'Not for a couple of years. We— Oh…wow. Oh… my…' Tara trailed off, looking down the corridor. 'Oh, my goodness.' She fanned her hand in front of her face. 'What a man.'

'What's happening?'

Dane was happening, Mariel realised when he appeared in the doorway. Filled the doorway.

And he really *was* happening.

At least she thought it was Dane. Except this man had neatly trimmed *short* hair, and a clean-shaven face, and he was wearing a *tux* and carrying the biggest bunch of pink and white roses she'd ever seen.

Beyond the door she thought she heard a couple of feminine sighs, but she was too busy taking in the view, trying to calm her racing heart, and backing up to the bed before her legs gave way to pay any attention.

His eyes fused with hers like an electrical short-circuit. Held. Without breaking contact, he closed the door with one shiny new shoe. It shut with a heavy thud. He walked to the side of the bed, went down on one knee before her. His tux—her own design, she noted through the haze—was dusted with a fine sheen of rain, his hair damp. The scent of misted roses and some sexy new aftershave wafted to her nose.

But it was the naked emotion in his eyes that nearly did her in. This man knew her, often better than she did herself. He'd travelled childhood's tumultuous journey with her, shared the ups and downs of their teenage years. They could argue the point till the sun switched off and still not give in. He knew her idiosyncrasies and delighted in holding them up to her.

But in the end he respected her, gave her space when she needed it, let her be herself. He understood her because they came from the same place.

He was the only man she'd ever truly loved.

And he was kneeling before her like some knight to his lady. Like one of her teenage fantasies. Her heart was blossoming with so many emotions she didn't know how she could possibly hold them all in. But a thread of pain ran through the beauty.

'Dane, I have to tell y—'

'Not a word,' he said. 'Not. One. Word.'

He laid the flowers aside and pulled a shiny box from his pocket, opened it and held it up for her inspection.

A solitaire diamond as big as her little fingernail sparkled in the light. Heavens. 'Dane…' She pressed her lips together to stop the tremble. 'What are you doing?'

'My God, woman, what do you think I'm doing?' His voice boomed in the small room.

'There are sick people here,' she whispered.

His expression darkened. 'And I might very well be one of them if you don't let me get this over with. I told you to zip it. Mariel…'

He took the ring between finger and thumb and held it up to her. 'This ring's like you. It's bright and beautiful and one of a kind. And it'll be the one you hand down to our oldest grandchild.'

Grandchildren? Shock struck her speechless for one stunned moment, then a wave of happiness rolled up and swamped her. 'Do you mean that?' she whispered.

'I was never more serious. But that's down the track a bit. When you've recovered.' He smiled briefly, then reached for her hand and slid it on. 'Perfect fit. Like us, Queen Bee.'

Tears sprang to her eyes. 'I have to tell you—'

But he stifled her words with a finger. 'Not done yet. I love you. I always have. I always will. I've loved you since that first day at school, when I saw you standing in the sandpit in your new brown and yellow uniform. The Queen Bee surrounded by her faithful swarm of little boys.'

'You marched up and pulled the ribbon off my pigtail.'

'I wanted your attention.'

'And you got it, all right. I beat the living daylights out of you *and* got my ribbon back.'

His smile faded. 'When you told me you were pregnant I couldn't come to terms with it. I couldn't imagine being a father. I needed time. I didn't give a thought to the fact that you'd be needing time, too. That we could have supported each other the way we always have and got through it together.'

'Yes, we could have. We should have. You shut yourself off, but I should have tried harder to reach you.' Mariel reached out to stroke his smooth, tight jaw, then patted the bed beside her in invitation.

'You know my take on commitment,' he said, rising. He sat beside her and searched her eyes. 'But I know now that my heart was waiting for you. It just didn't relay the information to my brain.'

She shook her head. 'I always loved you. Even ten years ago when I saw you with Isobel I loved you. And hated you.'

His smile sobered as quickly as it had come. 'You were so set on going overseas. I didn't want to stop you from doing what you needed to do. And I was afraid to start anything with you, to show you how I felt, because everyone I loved either left or turned their back on me.'

She fingered his newly cropped hair. 'You've made a start with your father, Dane.'

'We've still got a long way to go. But I've got some

ideas that I want to discuss with you. Later.' He cupped her face in one large warm palm. 'We weren't ready ten years ago. You needed to follow your dreams first and so did I. But children…'

He shook his head, and in his expression Mariel saw the old wounds which had never quite healed.

'After my own miserable childhood I was convinced family wasn't for me. I was wrong. I want you to have my babies. I want to watch them grow inside you, see their first smile, be there when they take their first steps. Support them as they grow to adulthood. We can have more babies, Mariel, if you'll marry me.'

She smiled at him through a mist. 'I guess I'll have to marry you, Dane, and as soon as possible—because I want this baby to be born to loving parents who've made a lifetime commitment.'

His eyes widened, then dropped to where Mariel's hand touched her belly. 'Run that by me again—the bit about this baby.'

'I'm still pregnant.' She sniffed, unable to contain her emotion any longer. 'I saw it on a monitor. It's real, Dane.'

Grasping both her hands, he jack-knifed off the bed. 'You're going to marry me and you're having my baby!'

The sound of clapping issued through the door as he hauled her against him and kissed her. And, wow, what a kiss. She cupped his smooth jaw and ran her fingers over his short-cropped hair. Again. To acquaint herself with its feel.

At last they came up for air, and she stepped back so she could admire the man who'd walked North Terrace on a weekday morning wearing a tux and carrying flowers. The man who'd changed for her. 'You are *so* the man for me. You always were. I have everything—a man who loves me, a baby on the way and a promising business.'

'Ah, yes, speaking of which… Let's get out of here. I have something to show you before the press catches on to all this news. There's a cab waiting at the service entrance.'

The taxi took them to a street near the centre of town.

Mariel walked with him until Dane stopped and gestured to an empty shop just off Rundle Mall. 'What do you think?'

'About what?'

He produced a key, handed it to her. 'Your new business premises.'

'Oh. Oh, goodness.' Her fingers trembled so much she couldn't get the key in the lock.

He grinned, took the keys from her and did the honours. 'I think this is where we started not so long ago. Fumbling with keys.'

The smell of fresh paint and new beginnings met Mariel as she stepped inside.

'There's a big room out back for supplies, tailors, anything else you want,' Dane said beside her.

'It's beautiful. Just beautiful.' Honey-toned wooden counters gleamed. Empty racks lined the walls. A large shiny window faced the mall, waiting for the shop's name to be painted on it.

She spun a circle in the middle of the newly fitted-out room. 'I can't wait to move in. When did you do all this?'

'Finished yesterday. It was hard trying to keep it a secret and organise it from up north. That's why I had to go out the other night. There was a problem with the lighting.'

'Ah… The night you asked me to trust you.'

'And you did.'

'Thank you. For this…' She swept her hand to encompass the room. 'And this.' She took his hand, pressed it against her belly.

Dane pulled her tightly against him. 'Let's go home,' he murmured into her hair. 'I want to celebrate our good fortune in *our* bed.'

She smiled, listening to the gallop of his heart against her ear. 'Yes, let's go home.'

EPILOGUE

Two years later

'COME on, Danny, walk to Grandpa.'

Mariel smiled as fourteen-month-old Daniel Huntington the Fourth's toothy grin widened. His chubby
hands were outstretched as he toddled the last few steps
into the waiting arms of his grandfather.

Since Dane's father had moved in with them the pair
had become inseparable. Mariel couldn't have been
happier. Dane and his father had been given a second
chance, and they'd grabbed hold of it with both hands.

Family, she thought. A blessing. She smoothed a
hand over her still-flat belly. This time she wanted a
girl, to even things up a bit. As for Dane—he was too
happy about her announcement to care.

'You sure you'll be okay, Dad?' Dane asked as he
shrugged into his suit jacket.

'You're only a few minutes and a phone call away.
Of course we're all right—aren't we, Danny boy?'

The child gurgled up at him happily.

'He'll be fine.' Mariel opened her compact, checked her make-up. 'They'll both be fine. Stop worrying.'

'This is the first time we've left them together,' Dane murmured.

'He can change a nappy as well as you, if not better. Come on. The restaurant booking's for eight and I don't want to be late. Justin and Cass have got news, I just know it. Oh… Have you read my review?' she asked nonchalantly as she adjusted his silk tie to her satisfaction.

He didn't even seem to mind her female fussing. 'I have. Twice.'

'Read it again. Aloud, so I know.'

Fashion designer Mariel Davenport's latest showing last night has been hailed by the fashion industry as a rousing success. Her label, Dane, is at the cutting edge of men's fashion, with its subtle French influence and effervescent use of colour.

Ms Davenport's advice: 'A man should stay true to himself rather than following fashion blindly. My husband is a prime example.'

That's why Dane Huntington is often seen in worn jeans while sporting the latest in cashmere jumpers.

He's the luckiest man in Adelaide.

Twinkling eyes lifted to meet hers. '*That's* why you wanted me to read it aloud.'

She tilted her nose at him. 'No. I just wanted to hear it again, Mr Luckiest Man. You don't need to read it to know it's true.'

'You're right. This time.'

'I'm always right.' She leaned in for a quick kiss. 'That's why you married me.'

His eyes danced with laughter and he yanked her back for an encore. 'No. That's why you married me.'

Coming Next Month

in **Harlequin Presents®**. Available July 27, 2010.

Coming Next Month

in **Harlequin Presents® EXTRA**. Available August 10, 2010.

HARLEQUIN®

A Romance

FOR EVERY MOOD™

Spotlight on
─ Heart & Home ─

Heartwarming romances
where love can happen
right when you least expect it.

See the next page to enjoy a sneak peek
from Harlequin® American Romance®,
a Heart and Home series.

CATHHHAR10

Five hunky Texas single fathers—five stories from Cathy Gillen Thacker's LONE STAR DADS *miniseries. Here's an excerpt from the latest,* THE MOMMY PROPOSAL *from Harlequin American Romance.*

"I hear you work miracles," Nate Hutchinson drawled. Brooke Mitchell had just stepped into his lavishly appointed office in downtown Fort Worth, Texas.

"Sometimes, I do." Brooke smiled and took the sexy financier's hand in hers, shook it briefly.

"Good." Nate looked her straight in the eye. "Because I'm in need of a home makeover—fast. The son of an old friend is coming to live with me."

She was still tingling from the feel of his warm palm. "Temporarily or permanently?"

"If all goes according to plan, I'll adopt Landry by summer's end."

Brooke had heard the founder of Nate Hutchinson Financial Services was eligible, wealthy and generous to a fault. She hadn't known he was in the market for a family, but she supposed she shouldn't be surprised. But Brooke had figured a man as successful and handsome as Nate would want one the old-fashioned way. *Not that this was any of her business...*

"So what's the child like?" she asked crisply, trying not to think how the marine-blue of Nate's dress shirt deepened the hue of his eyes.

"I don't know." Nate took a seat behind his massive antique mahogany desk. He relaxed against the smooth leather of the chair. "I've never met him."

"Yet you've invited this kid to live with you permanently?"

"It's complicated. But I'm sure it's going to be fine."

Obviously Nate Hutchinson knew as little about teenage

boys as he did about decorating. But that wasn't her problem. Finding a way to do the assignment without getting the least bit emotionally involved was.

Find out how a young boy brings Nate and Brooke together in THE MOMMY PROPOSAL, coming August 2010 from Harlequin American Romance.